Bob Bridges

an apocalyptic fable

the end of the human species • spiritual evolution • hot cocoa
nuclear disaster • rise of the roaches • y2k • sunworshipping

☢ ⚛ ☢ ⚛ ☢

Penny Perkins

CHROME • DECO PRESS

Excerpt on page 5, "certain maxims of archy", *from* ARCHY AND
MEHITABEL by Don Marquis. Copyright © 1927 by Doubleday, a
division of Bantam, Doubleday, Dell Publishing Group, Inc. Used
by permission of Doubleday, a division of Random House, Inc.

Excerpt on page 12, "The Moth in the Machine" used by permission:
Copyright © 1998 by Daniel Kohanski
from THE PHILOSOPHICAL PROGRAMMER by Daniel Kohanski
Reprinted by permission of St. Martin's Press, Incorporated

For more information on BOB BRIDGES, including ordering
information, visit the Web site: www.bobbridges.com

FIRST EDITION

Cover and book design by
Alpha/Omega Text/Image Services
www.alphaomega1.com

Library of Congress Catalog Card Number: 99-63286.

ISBN 0-9672304-0-3

Manufactured in the United States of America
10 9 8 7 6 5 4 3 2 1

for
Elizabeth Terra Gaia
and all those who promote
her perseverance, prosperity, and perpetuity

Human life is threatened by many perils that are all working together and coming to a head at about the same time. I am one of those scientists who finds it hard to see how the human race is to bring itself much past the year 2000.

— Dr. George Wald, Nobel Prize-Winning Scientist
Apocalypse 2000

When the activity of an organism favors the environment as well as the organism itself, then its spread will be assisted; eventually the organism and the environmental change associated with it will become global in extent. The reverse is also true, and any species that adversely affects the environment is doomed; but life goes on.

— Dr. James Lovelock, Scientist
The Ages of Gaia: A Biography of Our Living Earth

The Earth is a beautiful place, but it has a pox called man.

— Friedrich Nietzsche

CONTENTS

PART 2: HIGH NOON
THE DIALOGUE
39

A Dialogue Between Bob and a Creature from the Distant Future, Wherein the Creature Recounts the Demise of Bob's Species and Requests that Bob Join the Creature in Its Own Civilization to Help Decipher Some Mysteries of the Present Time

PART 3: SUNSET
A TRIP TO MINNESOTA
79

Chapter 1:
Bob Agrees to Return to the Distant Future **81**

Unexpected Memory Interruption #1:
A Childhood Car Trip **85**

Chapter 2:
The Hospitality House **89**

Unexpected Memory Interruption #2:
Welcome to *Bleakerville!* **102**

Chapter 3:
A Walk Around Town **113**

Unexpected Memory Interruption #3:
Fast Food, Anyone? **122**

Chapter 4:
Bob Becomes a Celebrity in an Alien Culture **127**

Unexpected Memory Interruption #4:
Pining for the Beauty of Movie Stars **141**

Part 1 :
Meet Bob Bridges

☢ ⚛ ☢ ⚛ ☢

Chapter 1:
Meet Bob Bridges

Meet Bob Bridges.

Bob is 36. He is gainfully employed. He lives alone. He has good friends. He likes movies. He votes. He even works out on the weekends. In all, a rather likable, quiet kind of guy.

But Bob has a problem. A big problem. Bob has a problem with bugs.

Bugs rule Bob's life. Maybe they always have. He had a dream as a child. He awoke—or so he thought—from a bad dream only to find himself inside a worse one, with a starring role as a bug at the bottom of the ocean. But the trouble wasn't that he was a bug, *per se* —bugs that are pure bugs don't mind being bugs, because they have no Other-bug consciousness to tell them that there's something else to be besides a bug. No, the problem in the dream was that, even though he had the body of a bug, Bob also had the full consciousness of a human being. The consciousness of a full-grown adult human harboring a pantheon of passions, ambitions, memories, and desires. But he was in a mollusk's body. A shell, really. Nothing more than a shell. And to make matters far worse, Bob-the-Bug was sitting—in the dark, in the frigid, utter darkness—at the bottom of the ocean, with the full weight and pressure of all the sea's strata bearing down upon him. But that smothering press from the last layer of the ocean was nothing like the full weight and girth of his own bulging consciousness. And when Bob-the-Bug-with-the-Full-Consciousness-of-a-Human realized this—that he was a bug with a human's mind trapped on the bottom of the ocean—then the dream ended in a startling implosion, the logical conclusion of the paradox of his existential crisis.

But now Bob has a different problem with bugs. Not like the one in the dream. In fact, he doesn't even remember that dream. It will come back to him, though, later, after a significant event happens in this story. But for now, that dream—like his previous lives as a bug —are safely tucked away, in the undredged sands of his unconscious.

That's good for Bob—and for you, too, as an observer of Bob —because otherwise he wouldn't do what he's just about to do.

Real-World Interruption #1:
A Poem¹ from an Insect's View

insects have
their own point
of view about
civilization a man
thinks he amounts
to a great deal
but to a
flea or a
mosquito a
human being is
merely something
good to eat

i do not see why men
should be so proud
insects have the more
ancient lineage
according to the scientists
insects were insects
when man was only
a burbling whatisit

                    archy the cockroach

¹ stanzas from "xii certain maxims of archy" from *archy and mehitabel* by Don Marquis, Anchor Books, Doubleday, 1927, reprinted paperback edition 1990. Used by permission.

Chapter 2:
Bob at the Office

It is the day after Labor Day 1998—a holiday that once had its roots in celebrating blue-collar industrial workers and that now merely provides an end-of-summer romp—and Bob makes his way to his desk at the office. He can hardly tell that there has been a holiday, because for him there has been none. While his working compatriots were getting their last sunburn of the season, Bob was craving lumbar support. He sat in his home office desk chair all weekend and wrestled with the screen.

Yes, no rest for Bob. Bob is busy. Busy as a beaver. And it's one heck of a dam that he's building.

Or unbuilding rather. You see, Bob is a computer programmer. And he is engaged in the great computing task of the late twentieth century. No, not calculating *pi* to the billionth place. No, not programming "Big Blue" to beat another round of human chess masters. No, not creating computer-generated dinosaurs for popular entertainment. Instead, Bob is on a religious quest, a search for the Binary Grail, and this grail comes in the shape of dates, of keeping track of time.

In other words, Bob Bridges—one of the brightest minds of his generation, one of the brightest minds in an industry that congratulates itself on its unusually bright minds—is working on what has become known as the Year 2000 Problem, or the "millennium bug," the Y2K bug, for short.

The Y2K bug. It's a rat's nest of a problem, one easy to explain and easy to understand, but impossibly difficult to fix, and it goes something like this:

Back in the ancient days of computer programming (say, the late 1950s) when programmers were first producing code on a widespread level for business and government computers, a tiny shortcut was created in writing dates. That is, instead of listing a year by its full four-number representation, a year was shortened to its last two digits. For instance, the year 1962 would be represented in code as "62" instead of "1962." Therefore, a date such as July 15, 1962, would be represented as "071562" and not its longer more accurate cousin "07151962."

At the time, no one suspected that the programs they were creating would be used even 10 years down the line, let alone 40 years, and the notion that "62" could stand for the sixty-second year in *any* century (not just the current century) never occurred to anyone. Or, if the problem did occur to them, the programmers thought they would be retired by then and not be personally affected.

Besides, in those days, computers were huge (they fit in a room, not on a desk) and memory space was extremely expensive. Used over millions of lines of code, the date shortcut saved space, and therefore money, and, for a while, everyone was very pleased with themselves.

Until, Orwellianly enough, 1984. That's when an article about the Y2K problem appeared in the magazine *Computer World*, a wake-up call that turned out to be the first published warning. But, as these things go, the author of the article was later fired by his managers, who became irritated by the insistence of their employee-turned-Cassandra crying that there was a ghost in the machine. So, for a few more years, Y2K was again ignored.

Until about 1990, that is. That's when a few more visionary folks (the managers who think in terms of decades and not just fiscal years or monthly reports) started to finally understand that software using the date shortcut may not be able to properly read dates after

1999, when the date "00" could be read as "1900" and not "2000."

The first widespread warnings went out then about the adverse effects of these millions of miscalculations, noting that the bug could cause a range of real-world mistakes—everything from the annoying, such as having the interest on your mortgage calculated for 70 years instead of 30, to the life-threatening, such as pacemakers run by internal computer chips that suddenly stopped pumping at the stroke of midnight on New Year's Eve.

Still, no one much heeded these ever-growing forewarnings until around 1995 when computers, while projecting five-year forecasts for corporations, began to grind to a halt. "Hey, there's something to this," folks began to concede. Another round of panic set in a few years later when credit cards with expiration dates past "00" began to crash the electronic cash registers of major department stores.

As the deadline of December 31, 1999 looms ever larger, the possibility of the "time bomb" of the Y2K bug exploding begins to sound less and less like science fiction, and more and more like technological fact.

As Bob and his employers well know, nearly every facet of contemporary life intersects with computers—banking, communications, government, business, utilities, medicine, transportation. Nothing is untouched. Even appliances, from coffeemakers to VCRs, are run by internal logic chips, mini-computers inside the mundane machines we rely upon to facilitate our daily lives.

What will happen *exactly* as a consequence of the Y2K miscalculation is subject to the contextual variations of the software and thus depends on each computer program and what aspect of our lives it intersects.

In the interim, there are literally billions of lines of code to be reviewed and billions and billions of embedded microchips to test and replace before the global-wide problem will be solved. As each day goes by, everyone understands more clearly that the task will never be finished by the deadline. The project at hand now is deciding what to focus on: Which programs are the priority? Which systems do we concentrate on to contain the damage? The operative word in the battle against the bug: *triage*.

Yes, it's a war—and a race against time. No one knows this better than Bob. Perhaps *only* Bob knows just how serious the situation is. And now it's up to him to make others understand the gravity of it all.

But is Bob up to the task? He should be. Remember: He's one of the best programmers in town.

In fact, Bob's a regular code fiend. And he specializes in computer languages designed in the mainframe era. Bob's a PASCAL poet, a BASIC bard, a FORTRAN fool, a one-man COBOL cabal. Economy of language is his middle name. And with his poetic economics, Bob writes beautiful code. Programmers swoon over it. It got him laid many times in graduate school. But more to the point, he loves writing it. Bob knows to the depths of his marrow that there is nothing so comforting as the precision of a million logical, Boolean commands being processed every second—for no other reason than because Bob wrought it so.

Bob writes the kind of code that makes computers sing. Now, Bob has never actually *heard* a computer sing. He's not schizophrenic, you understand. But he *imagines* what the happiness of computers crunching his elegant, efficient code sounds like. It sounds like the click of a shutter on an expensive camera. Like the lilt of Velcro lifting and latching. Those are some of Bob's favorite sounds. And if computers could purr, could make a noise at the beautiful logic of Bob's code, that's what they would sound like, he imagines. Like a shutter, like Velcro. Like love. Like the symphony of synapses popping in Bob's brain when an "If P, Then Q" rocket fires like a hot-wired haiku in rapid, stutter-step motion. Bob loves language, and he loves the precise language of code best of all.

Bob plies his amazing gifts in the service of the company he works for, SIMS, Inc.—Super Information Management Systems, Incorporated—with its international headquarters right here in Bob's adopted hometown of Minneapolis, Minnesota.

At SIMS, Inc., Bob is not just a cog in the machine. Bob *programmed* the machine. And he's a star, a regular digerati supernova. Only lately, he hasn't felt like such a star. He hasn't been getting the respect he feels he deserves. He has begun to understand something—something big about his work and his world—and he has hinted at the consequences of it with Management. But Management doesn't want to hear it. It's not that what Bob has discovered isn't true —it's just that his discovery doesn't go along with their corporate projections, completion timelines . . . not to mention the public relations strategy of their biggest client, the US government. Bob has been persistent, though—he has a bit of the bulldog in him, as well as the bug—and his persistence isn't making his superiors happy.

But Bob is smart. Too smart. And too stupid, too. Because now, after the avalanche of work he accomplished over the weekend, Bob knows his hypothesis—his worst fear—is true. And something must be done about it.

Even if Management doesn't want to...

Real-World Interruption #2:
An Excerpt[2] from a Computer Programming Book

CHAPTER 16: THE MOTH IN THE MACHINE

In September 1944, engineers testing the Mark I computer were puzzled when a section of the circuitry suddenly began misbehaving. After several hours of furious examination, they discovered that a moth had crawled into one of the relays, preventing it from making contact. From then on, whenever the director of the Mark I project asked why something was not proceeding according to schedule, he was told it was because they were "debugging the computer." This was not the first use of "bug" to mean an error—as far back as the 1920s, telephone company repairmen referred to insulation-eating insects as "bugs in the system"—but from that moment, the terms "bug" and "debugging" came to be identified with computers and computer programming.

Bugs, or errors, are the bane of a programmer's existence. We spend most of our careers locating and fixing bugs. Maurice Wilkes, director of the Cambridge EDSAC project, recalls the exact moment in June 1949 when he realized that "a good part of the remainder of my life was going to be spent in finding errors in my own programs."

[2] *The Philosophical Programmer: Reflections on the Moth in the Machine*, by Daniel Kohanski (St. Martin's Press, NY, 1998) pp. 159 and 160. Used by permission.

Chapter 3:
Bob Tells

B ob has been wrestling with his conscience all morning. He's been staring at an empty e-mail screen for more than an hour. He has something on his mind. He has something to say. In fact, he has already said it in other forums, but his bosses didn't want to hear it. Bob realizes that he will have to say it again, more forcibly. Much more forcibly.

Bob is not one to make threats. Idle or veiled or otherwise. So, just to make sure, he reviews his notes; he surveys the clarity of his thinking.

Yes, there is no mistaking it. His conclusions are faultless. He can no longer ignore the magnitude of his discovery.

Resolute in his convictions and determined in his righteousness, Bob sets out to send the MOTHER OF ALL E-MAILS to his boss. The dragon must be confronted. The consequences of not acting are simply too dear.

Subject: Year 2000 Compliance for DOD
Sent: 09/08/98 10:23 AM
From: Bob Bridges, bridges_b@simsinc.net
To: Robert Bruce, bruce_r@simsinc.net

Dear Robert,
        I am writing to you to express again my grave concerns regarding the Y2K bug faced by our biggest client, the US Department of Defense (DOD).

As you know, I have been periodically expressing my deep reservations regarding the catastrophic consequences of the Y2K bug in certain DOD software programs, particularly those that control and regulate nuclear weapons, nuclear warheads, and nuclear stockpiles.

What follows is a concerted, documented attempt to make crystal clear my concerns, supported by the testimony and observations of other industry experts.

The External Background

First of all, I direct your attention to the following facts, as compiled by Capers Jones in his seminal work, *The Year 2000 Software Problem: Quantifying the Costs and Assessing the Consequences* (1997), and paraphrased below:

The military has more software than any other government agency or corporation within the private sector, with more than 6 million separate software applications; more than 1,000 software sites; and more than 30 billion statements of code. [*The Year 2000 Software Problem*, Jones (Addison-Wesley), 1997, p. 52.]

Furthermore, according to Y2K consultant Edward Yourdon—coauthor with his daughter Jennifer of *Time Bomb 2000: What the Year 2000 Computer Crisis Means to You*—the programming languages used within the DOD are so obscure that many of them are not even used anywhere else. Specifically, the Yourdons note that DOD software has been written "in dozens of arcane programming languages that are no longer in current use—including high-level languages like Jovial, and low-level assembly languages for computer hardware that is no longer being manufactured." [*Time Bomb 2000*, Yourdon & Yourdon (Prentice Hall PTR) 1997, p. 253]

Thus, the difficulty in finding and training programmers to debug Y2K problems in DOD software is already a difficult task.

However, as you know, there is an additional problem: much of the DOD software is embedded in weapons and/or weapons command-and-control. Again, the Yourdons note that the consequences of the Y2K bug on DOD weapons could be catastrophic: "Planes, missiles, bombs, tanks, satellites, ships, air defense systems—and devices whose existence DOD has never admitted in public—all of these and more are controlled by, scheduled by, or interact with, date-sensitive computers." [*Time Bomb 2000*, Yourdon & Yourdon (Prentice Hall PTR) 1997, p. 254]

As you know, I personally have been spending the bulk of my waking hours on this problem. My research confirms that the DOD is *not* concentrating its resources on the weapons systems and appropriate support systems that are crucial to fix in order to avert a global nuclear catastrophe.

By my calculations—which, as you know, have been compiled using my top-security DOD clearance supplied specifically for SIMS contracts—the stockpiles of nuclear weapons alone, which are far greater than the government has indicated to the general public, are regulated and maintained by sensitive computers, many of which are decades old and all of which are run on software containing Y2K bugs.

Even if all programmers currently working on Y2K problems in *all* industries redirected their energies TODAY to review and resolve Y2K bugs in DOD software related to nuclear weapons, there would not be enough manpower and hours before the December 31, 1999 deadline to alleviate all problems.

This, of course, is the situation regarding nuclear weapons. When the similar situation is contemplated for biological weapons, conventional weapons, and classified weapons—all controlled and regulated by software containing Y2K bugs—the possibility of mass explosions, widespread human collateral damage, and global environmental destruction rings palpable.

Further exacerbating the problem is the little-heralded fact that the US DOD has clandestinely sold nuclear warheads and other weapons of mass destruction to foreign interests. [See FOIA requests 1995-002A and 1994-117C, attached.] Included for the price of the weapons was the software to maintain and deploy them —software which also contains the Y2K bug. Thus, we have a grave global situation before us: Even if we could neutralize all the software bugs associated with domestic weapons (which we cannot), we certainly cannot contain the Y2K bugs which affect US weapons that have been sold to foreign governments and independents.

This, of course, is all independent of the nuclear weapons and deployment software that have been independently developed and manufactured by foreign interests—which, again, also are riddled with Y2K compliance issues.

Furthermore, in addition to the specter of a nuclear weapons catastrophe, there are many other armament stockpiles which generate grave concerns as well. As an example, let us focus on just one other instance besides the nuclear warhead, i.e., the biological germ warhead.

The mother lode of germ warfare in this country is located at Fort Detrick in Frederick, Maryland where, according to *The New York Times*, "scientists, engineers, and technicians have worked to turn bacteria, fungi, viruses, and microbial toxins into 'products' meant to kill and incapacitate people in gruesome ways."[1] [see chapter endnote]

Although President Nixon purportedly ended the program in November 1969, top secret and unregulated work in this area has continued unabated ever since without public knowledge. In fact, after the US and Russia signed an international treaty in 1972 banning germ weapons and arms, both Moscow and Washington secretly redoubled their germ research and production. Furthermore, stockpiles of the already developed US germ warfare "products" remain cloistered and sequestered—some in deep freeze, some in more virulent states of activity. Of course, all these germ warfare stockpiles—like the heavily endowed stockpiles of conventional, petrochemical, and nuclear arms—are likewise controlled and regulated by computers infested with Y2K bugs.

That is the situation in this country. There are also similar germ "products" actively in production at various government and "free-agent" research centers and paramilitary compounds around the world. Recently, high-ranking government defectors from Moscow have confirmed that the Russian government has secretly produced hundreds of tons of anthrax, smallpox, and plague germs. And in Iraq, to name another major production source, Saddam Hussein's germ warfare program has grown enough pestilential microbes to kill everyone on the planet many times over.

Again, these foreign germ warfare programs are also controlled and maintained by computers, and, again, these computers are also subject to Y2K breakdowns. And, as a rule, other countries are even less prepared than the United States in addressing these critical Y2K issues.

If these nightmares were not enough—the virtual certainty of a global-wide nuclear and weapons meltdown following Y2K computer-related breakdowns, along with the release into the air and groundwater of hundreds of tons of killer microbes—we must also factor in the impact of leakage and meltdowns of the dozens of nuclear reactors currently in use throughout the world. Indeed, the Y2K bug is likewise inextricably interwoven in the massive systems of software that command and control the functioning of nuclear reactors throughout the world.

Imagine hundreds of Chernobyls, dozens of Three Mile Islands, and untold numbers of Love Canal waste sites—all arriving, all detonating during the same period.

However, we may not need to wait until January 1, 2000 for these meltdowns. Some of the nuclear reactor catastrophes are likely to occur months earlier, and not all need necessarily be Y2K related. For instance, the ITAR-Tass news agency, Russia's official press, recently reported that Ukraine's Nuclear Regulation Administration refused to shut down the ailing Chernobyl facility for needed repairs. The aging nuclear power plant has exhibited many malfunctions since its main reactor was destroyed in the infamous 1986 explosion and fire disaster. Moreover, in the United States, where 40% of the energy for the northeastern seaboard comes from nuclear power plants, the Nuclear Energy Regulatory Commission may be faced with shutting down all plants in July 1999 which are not guaranteed to be Y2K compliant. The loss of electricity alone for such a wide-spread area would likely lead to other natural and civil disasters.

So far in this analysis, I have barely touched upon the embedded microprocessor chip problem. Ultimately, this aspect of the Y2K problem may prove as lethal as the software problems. Given the severity of our main topic of discussion, however, I will not delve into the embedded chip issue in detail here [see my previous memo of 03/04/1998, cited below, for further discussion]. However, one aspect I am deeply concerned with, and will briefly mention, is the possibility of massive satellite failure, particularly of the Global Positioning System (GPS) guidance satellites, which are critical to military operations. As the embedded chips in these and other satellites fail, it is nearly certain that these dozens of orbiting objects will crash back to Earth, causing a meteor-like bombardment on a scale never before witnessed in the history of mankind. Of course, many of these satellites are powered with radioactive fuels which would poison large tracts of the Earth, in addition to causing destructive explosions, upon impact.

But let us return to the main topic of this communication: widespread nuclear missile detonation as a result of the operational failure of command and control computers. While the Y2K problem is foremost in our minds now as the culprit of such failures, we must keep in mind that other factors may also interrupt computer control of nuclear warheads, including, for instance, loss of electricity, earthquakes, civil unrest, or terrorism abetted by spying. Thus, this potential crisis of detonation cannot be overstated as mere theory or conjecture. In fact, my exhaustive research, aided by my top security clearance, has enabled me to pinpoint specific nuclear missile silos throughout the continental United States that are most vulnerable to various software problems, including the Y2K problem. Furthermore, I have been able to ascertain to a greater than 95% level of accuracy which of these pinpointed sites will likely detonate when Y2K problems are neither addressed nor completely eradicated before the encroaching deadline.

One such site, situated in the Ozark Mountains of Missouri, deserves particular attention because of 1) its proximity to an enormous underground water table which feeds directly into the Mississippi River and 2) its proximity to an active underground fault line which runs through the Ozarks and into southern Illinois. Thus, because of its geographic location, this particular missile silo, when detonated by general software failures and/or the Y2K computer error, will affect a much larger geographic area and many more population centers than it might at first inspection because of its domino effect of poisoning a large water source and triggering earthquakes along a far-reaching fault line.

The worst piece of news about this particular site is that, as one of the oldest silo sites in the country, it is run by computer hardware that is no longer manufactured. Moreover, the software run on these machines are predominantly low-level assembly languages; unfortunately, there are virtually no qualified programmers left who understand such programs.

Even if we started *today* to train programmers in this archaic language there would not be enough time for even 10,000 programmers to review, rewrite, and test an updated program before the Y2K deadline. This is because the software represented in that one silo in the heart of the Ozarks constitutes more than 1 billion lines of programming code.

Given such insurmountable odds, I feel it is necessary to state the obvious and warn that the ensuing Y2K nuclear crisis is absolutely unlike the crisis in a typical "disaster" movie. For in our world, there will be no muscular savior—no Last Action Hero—to enter at the last moment and save the day. It is clear that it is *too late* to solve the problem merely from a *software* standpoint.

Therefore, since we have neither the time nor the manpower to avert this problem in terms of software, we must do the only responsible thing and alert the government (our client) and the public (our fellow citizens) to the impending catastrophe, so that preparations may begin to save as many lives as possible.

I believe that the only way we may survive this crisis as a society is to wage a **MASSIVE GLOBAL DISARMAMENT**—that is, every weapon controlled by or connected with a computer must be **DISARMED** before the December 31, 1999 deadline.

It will be less costly and much quicker to simply disassemble stockpiles of weapons of mass destruction than to try to ensure the Y2K compliance of software systems which control their detonation.

LET ME REPEAT: AT THIS POINT IN TIME, THE ONLY POSSIBLE SOLUTION FOR SAVING OUR WORLD IS BY MASS GLOBAL DISARMAMENT AND THE DESTRUCTION OF WEAPONS STOCKPILES THE WORLD OVER.

This is the only option available to ensure the

continuation of society as we now enjoy it. I urgently request a meeting so that we may begin preparation for a coordinated series of announcements to government and public channels.

I do not believe it is histrionic to allege that the very fate of life on this planet may hinge on our responsive, and responsible, actions to this clear and present danger.

However, I am convinced that, working together, the people of the world can circumvent this self-created, life-threatening problem. The only chance, though, is to begin action NOW.

The Internal Background

I have brought these matters to your attention via e-mail, memo, and/or personal conversation on several occasions, including the following dates when I took notes about our interactions:

    10/01/1997 — staff lounge
    12/15/1997 — staff meeting
    03/04/1998 — internal memo
    06/18/1998 — follow-up e-mail
    07/15/1998 — conference with superiors
    08/05/1998 — dispute by water cooler
    08/29/1998 — dispute re: my evaluation

There are also a number of other occasions when I did not keep formal notes.

During each instance, your response has been steadfast: avoidance, denial, evasion, minimizing, and trivializing. This matter can no longer go unheeded. We must approach our superiors and we must alert our clients and our country to the grave dangers that lie ahead.

If no such appropriate response is forth-coming from you, I will be forced to take matters into my own hands, possibly involving outside legal and media representatives.

I eagerly await your response.

Sincerely,
Bob Bridges

Bob reads over his message after he finishes writing it, and then with great conviction and moral certitude presses the "send" button on his e-mail browser program. He hopes that he will get a more enthusiastic response this time from his boss now that he has laid out the argument in undeniable detail.

In the meantime, Bob does the only thing he knows how to do right now—he applies his immense talents to the great, unending task that stretches out before him: debugging the Y2K problem from the DOD software program that currently resides in his "in" box.

And just who is this Bob? This Bob who warns like Cassandra and then, like Sisyphus, rolls the insuperable rock of debugging up the hill of Y2K compliance?

This is Bob — just some nice, likable guy, trying to alert people to the dangers that lie ahead. This is Bob — just some guy trying to do his job, while being thwarted by the people above him, dumb bastards who've risen to their level of incompetence and who get paid twice as much as he does and who don't know one-tenth of what he does or how he does it.

That's who Bob is. Just some nice guy trying to do his job in spite of the stupidity of his superiors.

Ultimately, that's exactly who Bob is. A worker unappreciated. A cog in the machine, after all.

Someone, perhaps, not entirely unlike you.

[1] [Editor's Note: See, "Once He Devised Germ Weapons: Now He Defends Against Them," by William J. Broad and Judith Miller in *The New York Times*, 11/03/1998, F1 at col. 2.]

Real-World Interruption #3:
Unsolicited E-mail about Y2K Solutions

Subject: Y2K Solution!
Date: Tue, 27 Oct 1998 07:00:30
From: <informant@freeyellow.com>
To: <friend@public.com>

10/27/98

Y2K Solution!
8 Pine Circle Dr., Silicon Valley, Calif.

OTC Company "TCFG" 21 st. Century Frontier Group has through several members of their administrative research department leaked vital information about their companies [sic] efforts.

Everyone was tight lipped [sic] and interviews were refused, and through un-named sources we have learned that the technology and software solution are in the process of being patented!

In over 1,640 trials, using various data systems, the use of the new technology and software solved the Y2K problem 100% of the time.

This small publicly traded company "TCFG" which is just 3 years old is through various sources now negotiating with the "Big Boys"!

"TCFG" — the letters to look for!

Chapter 4:
Bob Gets Punished

A few hours later, when Bob returns from the company cafeteria with his lunch to eat at his desk, he sees that the "in" box of his e-mail browser contains a new message.

With equal parts hope and trepidation, Bob puts down his vegetable pita wrap and hurriedly opens the following reply from his boss:

Subject: RE: Year 2000 Compliance for DOD
Sent: 09/08/98 12:25 PM
From: Robert Bruce, bruce_r@simsinc.net
To: Bob Bridges, bridges_b@simsinc.net

Dear Bob:

It is important to emphasize that you are a programmer of extraordinary talent, energy, dedication, and enthusiasm. For this, we offer our gratitude, respect, admiration, and regard.

Indeed, these sentiments will certainly be the ones that we will relate when your prospective employers approach us for references.

You see, your belligerence on a subject that—by your own admission—has already repeatedly been addressed and dismissed for lack of substantiating evidence, has grown tiresome to the point of insubordination. Given the task that lies before this corporation— providing our clients and the US government with the most level-headed and task-oriented programmers available to tackle the substantial, but manageable, Y2K problem—it is clear that you no longer fit into the mission and goals of this company.

As a result, your employment with SIMS, Inc. has been terminated (effective immediately), your DOD security clearance has been revoked, and a company lawyer will be present in your office at 2:00 PM this afternoon to oversee the removal of personal artifacts from your desk and office. At this time, you will also be obliged to return your office keys and company parking sticker.

We wish you the best of luck in your future endeavors.

Sincerely,
R. Bruce
Vice President of Operations

P.S. Please note that public disclosure of the content of any of your work while at SIMS, Inc., including the substance of your e-mails, constitutes a violation of the terms of your employment contract, specifically your confidentiality clauses and your non-compete clauses. Moreover, public disclosure of any DOD work-related matter also violates several Federal laws and will result in your immediate arrest and incarceration.

Real-World Interruption #4:
A Government Warning

SEVERE SPACE STORMS WILL ARRIVE AROUND 1/1/00

ATMOSPHERIC DISRUPTIONS IN 2000 COULD INTERFERE WITH SATELLITE, COMMUNICATION SYSTEMS

<http://www.ntgov.com/gcn/gcn/1998/october19/33.htm>
By Gregory Slabodkin, GCN Staff

(Government Computer News) October 19, 1998— Computer crashes are not the only threat to military and civilian systems come the year 2000. Air Force experts and other government scientists have concluded that violent electromagnetic space storms will wreak havoc on systems at about the same time that the unfixed date code fails.

"We're going to have a huge storm [about] Jan. 1, 2000, so people won't know what to blame [the catastrophe] on," said Ernie Hildner, director of the National Oceanic and Atmospheric Administration's (NOAA) Space Environment Center in Boulder, Colorado. The center's Space Weather Operations, operated by NOAA and the Air Force, issues extraterrestrial event alerts to government and industry scientists hourly, much as the National Hurricane Center issues tropical storm or hurricane alerts.

Solar and geomagnetic events such as ion bombardments and explosions on the surface of the Sun can damage or knock out satellite transmissions, hamper navigation systems, cut electric power, and bring down telephone systems.

Unlike the year 2000 problem, space weather is a natural phenomenon that occurs in 11-year cycles. During the cycles, powerful geomagnetic storms generated by the Sun spew bursts of high-energy particles and clouds of ionized gas that can damage satellites and affect the Earth's magnetic field.

Sunspots, flares, filaments, coronal holes, and mass ejections emanating from the Sun throw off bursts of electromagnetic particles, radiation, and solar wind. Geomagnetic storms occur when blasts of solar wind bend and stretch the Earth's magnetic field.

The latest solar cycle—Cycle 23—is expected to reach its maximum strength around 2000, far surpassing the strength of its predecessor, Hildner said.

Geomagnetically induced currents from space weather can be picked up by power lines and disable transformers, Hildner said. Solar Cycle 22 in 1989, for instance, left more than 6 million people in Quebec, Canada, without electric power for 12 hours, he said.

Chapter 5:
Bob Goes on a Depressive Eating & Drinking Binge

Bob stumbles into his apartment, lugging a box of "personal artifacts"—a few framed photographs, a sickly African violet, and some research files—that he managed to salvage from his desk before being kicked out by SIMS, Inc. security personnel.

He walks straight into the kitchen, dumps the box on the counter, and lets out a heavy sigh. He steps over to the refrigerator and pulls out a beer before dialing the phone and ordering a pizza for home delivery. He's definitely not going out tonight. Tonight, Bob is staying in and licking his wounds—along with his mozzarella-soaked fingertips. He cannot believe they fired him. He cannot believe they wouldn't listen to him. So tonight he is staying in to listen to himself, to listen to the gulp of his throat as he eats an entire cheese pizza and drinks a six-pack of beer.

But Bob's no slob, even in his disheartened and depressed state. So, he turns on the kitchen radio to a classical music station that plays entire CDs before interrupting with liner notes and weather updates. Then he clears off the table, sets a matching placemat and napkin for himself, puts out a knife and fork, and then finally pours his beer into one of the frosted mugs he has lined up in the freezer.

If the truth be told, Bob's not much of a drinker. The frosted mugs are mostly for his niece Lauren who gets a big kick out of drinking her root beer out of them. But he does usually keep a six-pack of brown bottles in the refrigerator in case friends unexpectedly stop by and would like to wash down some chips and salsa (which Bob also keeps on hand for guests) with a little brewski. Mind you now, Bob has never actually uttered the word "brewski"—he thinks the term was outlawed at his college fraternity at the prestigious engineering school he attended—but he does try out the word in his mind every once in a while when making a goof on himself and his quiet, mature lifestyle.

And, just to prove the point of how civilized he is and how well he is taking his firing—Bob is a pillar of strength in adversity— he takes a short walk out his kitchen's back door, across the back porch, and down the steps to his perennial garden. Much to his delight, there is still a group of daisies in bloom—the purplish ones, his favorites— which he cuts with the Chinese scissors he brought out with him just in case.

As he snips a bloom from a stem, he remembers the passage about daisies that he memorized from his family's 1973 Funk & Wagnalls New Encyclopedia (the same encyclopedia he used to end- lessly lose himself in when his father was in one of his moods): "The daisy is not a single flower, but rather a composite of a center cluster of disk flowers surrounded by ray flowers." Bob loves the daisy and all the daisy-like composite flowers best because he thinks all of life is like that—nothing single in itself existing, but rather composites of existence clustering around various centers of activity.

Sometimes the daisy could be like a family, he thinks, like the way his grandmother was the center cluster that held together the surrounding rays of relatives. No one even realized that there was an organization to this family cluster at all, until his grandmother died and then they all went their separate ways—arguing each year where the holiday dinners would be held and who would be invited to come —like composite petals wilting and dropping off, one by one.

The daisy seems like such a simple flower—only something so simple and pure could stay fresh for so long, no?—and yet Bob knows that the complexity of its makeup is hidden in its multiple petal paths. In fact, Bob knows that composite flowers, like the daisy, are among the most advanced flowers on the planet, the most recently evolved. And somehow, given the complexity of his work and the simplicity of getting fired from it, Bob finds enormous comfort in bringing into his kitchen a late-season, composite daisy to garnish his dinner table in a small vase.

At last, all his preparations done, Bob sits down at the table to do nothing other than drink his beer and wait for his pizza to arrive —his emotions buzzed and buzzing, the sorrow and anger not yet coagulating into precise lumps of feeling.

While waiting, naturally, Bob thinks about his day, and his train of thought from daisies to families eventually takes him back to his work. For it seems to him that working on the Y2K bug and trying to alert others about the impending disasters arising from it is a lot like telling a family secret. It's as if a clandestine family of programmers and computer geeks had slowly overtaken every aspect of contemporary society. That in itself might be bad enough, depending on your perspective, but then it gets worse. For there was a little dysfunction in the family. A little problem with reconciling dates. And now there's going to be a full-blown accounting, a full-blown catastrophe because of it. But nobody wants to hear about that part. Nooooooooo. Nobody wants to pay attention to what Bob has been talking about; nobody wants to pay attention to this closely guarded secret at the heart of the clandestine family of computer programmers on which the entire industrialized world now depends.

But, really, it makes sense—now that Bob thinks about it more objectively from outside the confines of gainful employment. It's no wonder Management didn't want to hear what is going to happen, how their world is going to fall apart. Why, who are they going to sue in retaliation? The mountains will be in flames—the drinking water will be contaminated. The banks will fail, the stock market will crash, the cities will riot, and the backwaters—places where people have more guns than teeth—will take the issue of survival into their own 12-gauge hands.

Damn, no wonder I got fired, Bob suddenly realizes as he cracks open another beer. Why, who wants to hear a sad story like that? The End of The World. Only nuts and religious freaks talk about *that* story. And now Bob is one of them.

No wonder, Bob thinks. Certainly your Average Joe and Jane —and Bob counts himself in this group—don't want to know how completely our modern lives depend on computers and electronics. Every aspect of our daily lives—telephones, banks, grocery stores, restaurants, malls, hardware stores, gas stations, planes, trains, television, radio, newspapers, overnight mail, VCRs, pharmacies, hospitals, businesses, financial markets, and municipal, state, and government services—*even elevators for god's sake*—all hinge on an interrelated network of working, dependable computer systems or on independent embedded computer microchip processors. And, even worse, every aspect of our identity is marked by computers and computer systems—driver's license, checking accounts, credit cards, credit reports, criminal records, tax records, and on and on. Jesus, who wants to think about *that*?

Who wants to think about how some little machine invented within our own lifetimes now stands as the heart and linchpin of all of society?

Just like the center of the daisy, Bob thinks, with all these petals, these different aspects of society, surrounding it and depending on it.

If we think about this too hard, Bob realizes, then we're going to have to realize how our very survival, our very lives depend on a fallible little machine. A fallible little machine programmed by fallible little men who had no conception of the Frankenstein they were building 40 years ago and who had no foresight to realize that the party would all end on December 31, 1999, just because they neglected to write "1958" instead of the shorthand "58."

And, ultimately, who wants to think about what it would be like if the world indeed came to an end? Especially when there is laundry to do and children to care for and jobs to go to? Given the option of the concrete routines before us or the abstract horrors in front of us, human beings will always focus on the former.

So it goes, Bob thinks. So it goes.

Lucky for Bob's blood pressure—but equally unlucky for his cholesterol count—just then the doorbell rings. Bob gets up and answers the door, where a smiling young man in his twenties exchanges a cheese pie for a handful of singles from Bob's wallet.

The young man who delivers the pizza is named Michael. Michael O'Neal, in fact. He's a nice Irish Catholic boy, who's on an athletic scholarship to play basketball for the local college. Michael's brother just bought Luigi's Pizza Parlor from the former owner, Mr. Carmen Luigi, and Michael is doing his brother a favor by helping with deliveries during busy nights. Tonight is not busy—it's the first weekday after a big holiday—but Michael's brother is letting him work anyway because Michael could use the extra spending money for both his on- and off-campus extracurricular activities.

Bob doesn't know any of this, of course. Nor would he care if he did. Michael is just the pizza delivery guy to Bob. But Michael also bears the distinction of being the last human being that Bob will ever see or speak to again. And if Bob had known this, perhaps he would have taken a little more time to study the handsome boy's features, to gaze intently into his bright, blue eyes, and to thank him—*really* thank him—for delivering the pizza.

But instead of making a stronger connection with his fellow human being—whom, not surprisingly, Bob actually thinks about in the future frequently as his last contact with humanity—Bob barely notices Michael, wrapped up as he is in his hunger and his worries. So, Bob shuts the door and turns without another thought about Michael, and instead sets about his enterprise of eating the entire pizza and finishing off the rest of the beers while contemplating his troubles.

Bob, ever the task master, ever the pizza pie number cruncher and dwindling beer bottle counter, completes his self-appointed task amazingly well.

Bob, even though he is a trim man in his mid-thirties who doesn't drink much, packs away the entire pizza and drinks to the last foamy drop each of the six beers.

And then, his belly full, his veins racing, his eyelids drooping, Bob pushes aside his plate and rests his cloudy head in his arms on the table, just like he used to do in his college library when taking a little catnap inbetween chapters of some heavy, phrase-clunky engineering tome.

Real-World Interruption #5:
An AP Wire Story about Radioactive Bugs, October 1998

RADIOACTIVE INSECTS FOUND AT HANFORD NUCLEAR COMPLEX

(Associated Press) RICHLAND, WASHINGTON— Radioactive ants, flies, and gnats have been found at the Hanford nuclear complex in Richland, Washington, bringing to mind those Cold War-era B horror movies in which giant, mutant insects are the awful price paid for mankind's entry into the Atomic Age.

Although Hanford is working to eradicate its "hot" insects, officials said the radioactivity the pests carry is slight and no threat to neighboring communities.

The situation came to light in September when red harvester ants found underground near some old waste pipes were discovered to be radioactive. Then, earlier this month, workers discovered radioactive flying insects around cans where the staff's day-to-day nonradioactive garbage is thrown away.

Chapter 6:
Bob Hallucinates a Guest
(Or Does He?)

Bob has his face down, snoring away into an empty pizza box. He is dreaming in Panavision Technicolor® of a Cold War-era B horror movie in which giant, mutant insects attack an unsuspecting village full of peace-lovin', god-fearin' imbeciles, who do little more to protect themselves than run around willy-nilly on their skinny legs while waving their equally skinny arms and screaming.

Bob thinks this is no way for any self-respecting human-under-attack to react.

Just as he is about to change the channel on the old-fashioned TV set of his mind, from the distance, he hears someone calling his name.

"Bob. Bob. Wake up, Bob, you're dreaming."

The voice sounds exactly like his mother's.

Bob stirs his head slightly. He opens his eyes and greets the gray tones of the pizza box.

"Really, Bob, it's quite undignified for someone of your historical importance to fall asleep inside a pizza box."

Still looking into the aforementioned pizza box, Bob is surprised to hear the voice this time, because as far as he can tell he is awake and has stopped dreaming. And his significant experience with sleep and dreams—after all, he spends a third of his life perfecting the practice—tells him that mysterious dream-like voices (especially those sounding like his mother's), by all rights, should stop after he opens his eyes.

Bob lifts his head in the general direction of the voice and gets quite a start.

There, at the other end of the table, standing on its hind legs with its forelegs crossed in front of its underbelly like arms across a chest, is a cockroach.

Then a second remarkable thing happens: the cockroach opens its tiny mouth and discernible words come out of it.

"Really, Bob, I hadn't expected to find you like this. Perhaps I arrived a day early. Or a day late."

As if he has been hit by an electric shock, Bob flies back from the table, upsetting the chair. But, frankly, Bob is much more upset than the chair. Bob begins screaming and waving his hands while running around, looking desperately for something with which to kill the creature. On impulse, he grabs a thick copy of the latest *Wired* magazine that came in Saturday's mail—it is still on the counter waiting to be opened, ensconced in its plastic pouch—and takes his best swat at the bug.

"Jesus, Bob! What are you doing?!" The bug screams at him. "Stop it before somebody loses an eye!"

The creature scurries under the pizza box just before *Wired* can unplug its inner juices.

But Bob, hypnotized by terror, stands in a trance, swatting and swatting the table where the bug used to be.

The cockroach appears from under the pizza box on the other side of the table and yells to Bob the prophetic words, "Remember Gandhi, Bob! Remember Gandhi!"

Suddenly, Bob stops swatting the empty space where the cockroach used to be.

Yes, Bob stops trying to kill the creature with the magazine. But not because he is remembering Gandhi and Gandhi's proclamations of nonviolent resistance, but because he is suddenly thinking twice about killing a talking bug who knows his name.

Now, as far as Bob knows, bugs don't talk. Certainly none have addressed him by name, although he remembers an otter once who distinctly said "hello" to him in French when Bob was in Quebec on a camping trip with friends and had taken some of their acid on a dazzling afternoon.

Impatient with Bob's statuesque immobility, the cockroach interrupts Bob's slightly tangential train of thought.

"Thank you, Bob, for calming down. It's better for both of us."

Without thinking, Bob screams, "Stop calling me 'Bob'!"

Noting that the life-threatening maneuvers with the magazine have stopped, the creature rears up again on its hind legs and gestures pensively with an outstretched foreleg.

"But isn't that your name, Bob? I'm sure that's your name. I understand that 'Bob' is a diminutive for 'Robert,' your birth name. Would you prefer that appellation instead?"

The magazine, like the entire situation, is now completely out of Bob's hands and has dropped to the floor. Bob sits back down at the table and cradles his head in his hands. He speaks flatly, without looking at the creature.

"Yes, 'Bob' is my name. But you calling me by it bugs me."

The creature does its best interpretation of a smile, but, since its mouthparts move side-to-side and not up-and-down, the effect is somewhat eerie.

"Well, Bob, the last thing I want to do is bug you. Yessiree, Bob, that's the last thing I've come here for."

Bob looks up at the thing across his kitchen table which is incomprehensibly beaming at him and shaking. The roach is apparently laughing at him and waving its forelegs wildly.

This motion is particularly galling to Bob and he incongruously finds himself thinking, Great, I didn't just get visited by a talking roach, I had to get visited by an animated, gesticulating roach. Some picnic this is going to be.

And then, suddenly—with the unsullied truth hitting him like a bolt of midwestern lightning illuminating a midnight prairie—Bob surmises correctly that it's going to be a very long night.

Real-World Interruption #6:
**A Verbatim Notice from a Credit Card Company
on Y2K Compliance**

Your new Master Card is valid through 10/01.

Introducing your card for the 21st Century. Most Merchants are ready to accept cards with expiration dates of 2000 or later. If there is difficulty with your card, ask the Merchant to call for a verbal authorization. Then, please call our 24–hour Customer Satisfaction number and report the difficulty directly to us at our toll free number:
1-800-Y2K-SHOP.

Part 2 :
The Dialogue

(High
Noon)

A Dialogue Between Bob and a
Creature from the Distant Future,
Wherein the Creature Recounts the
Demise of Bob's Species and Requests
that Bob Join the Creature in Its Own
Civilization to Help Decipher Some
Mysteries of the Present Time

The Dialogue

Now the stage is set. Bob acquiesces to his situation, as bizarre as it might seem — but that is how Bob has survived as well as he has into adulthood, by adapting to the most unseemly of circumstances, by accepting the most unjust twists of fate. He tries not to take any of it personally. He just sucks in his breath and carries on as best he can. That, then, is what Bob does now.

He and the cockroach make themselves comfortable around Bob's kitchen table.

Then the cockroach takes the initiative and begins, thus hatching a discussion that flows headlong into the uncanny night.

Cock: Cheer up, Bob. It could be worse. I might not have come at all.

Bob: What *are* you?

Cock: We can get into that later. But for the time being, you may call me "Cock."

Bob: "Cock?"

Cock: Yes, my nickname. It's short for "Cockroach Hudson."

Bob: Terrific. Well, Cock Hudson, do you want to explain to me why it is you're dancing around on my kitchen table—and just what in Jesus' name you want?!

Cock: Really, Bob, no need for hysterics. First of all, I'm not dancing and second of all, the real question is what do *you* want?

Bob: I just want this day to start over.

Cock: I can't do anything about today. But I can do an awful lot about tomorrow.

Bob: Oh, really. Like what?

Cock: Like get you out of the mess you're in.

Bob: You mean being fired?

Cock: No, the bigger mess.

Bob: You mean being hunted down by secret government agents because I know their dirty little secret about Y2K meltdown?

Cock: No, the bigger mess. Don't personalize it so much, Bob.

Bob: You mean the world descending into chaos after all the computers crash?

Cock: Yes. And all that that entails. That's the mess I can help you with.

Bob: What will happen? Can you tell me?

Cock: I can only tell you the end result—which isn't good. But for now, let's just say it's a time of great uncertainty. And we all know that humans have a difficult time handling uncertainty.

Bob: If you know so much about all this—can't you do something about it?

Cock: I can . . . and I can't.

Bob: That would be poetic justice — it takes a bug to fix a bug!

Cock: What I mean is that I can alleviate *your* specific Y2K problems, but I can't fix the Y2K bug itself. It's far too late for that. And even if I could, I wouldn't.

Bob: Why? You like to see suffering on a mass level?

Cock: No. It's because it would interfere with the course of planetary history.

Bob: Oh, so you're one of those talking cockroaches who are a real stickler for historical accuracy. What are you, a slave to determinism?

Cock: Not exactly. It's more on the level of self-interest. You see, if I were to fix the Y2K bug—which, again, I can't—then I, and my entire civilization, will never exist.

Bob: Whoa, you're losing me, little buddy. There are others just like you somewhere?

Cock: Well, every creature in the universe is unique, Bob, but, yes, there are others *similar* to me somewhere, if not exactly just *like* me.

Bob: You're a real stickler for linguistical precision, too, aren't you?

Cock: We find that precision—as far as it's possible in an eternally fluxing and inextricably interdependent universe—is best.

Bob: And a philosopher to boot. Just what did I do to deserve this nightmare? Because, begging your pardon and all, I really, really hope this is all just a nasty hallucination brought on by too much cheese, sauce, and fermented yeast.

Cock: Oh, I don't mind. I'm not offended. Fear—not to mention confusion—is completely natural in your situation. I rather expected it.

Bob: Yeah, so as I was saying, just what did I do to deserve this visitation from a chattering insect?

Cock: Well, Bob, it's more like what you *didn't* do. It's about what all of you didn't do.

Bob: All of who?

Cock: You. Humans. Your "kind." Your "tribe." Your "people."

Bob: I get the picture.

Cock: I'm here today precisely because of what you as a species didn't do.

Bob: Is there a hidden camera here somewhere?

Cock: Jokes won't make the reality of it all go away, Bob. Although I completely understand and am somewhat sympathetic to the use of sarcasm as a defense mechanism in times of great emotional stress.

Bob: Thanks, Dr. Freud. But what do you want?

Cock: Essentially, I've come here today to ask you to come back with me.

Bob: Come back? Where? To the Bronx Zoo? The Island of Dr. Moreau? The bug cage of the lockdown ward at Bellevue?

Cock: Somewhere a little further than that.

Bob: Back to Bugville?

Cock: In a sense. Back to the future—where I come from.

Bob: The future? You come from the future?!

Cock: Yes. The very distant future. A future you can't even imagine—

and wouldn't want to even if you could.

Bob: All right. That's enough! You're starting to freak me out!

Cock: That's certainly not my intent.

Bob: Not your intent?! Then let's just recap the situation for a moment shall we?

Cock: You really should sit down. I think you'll be a lot more comfortable when we get to the difficult stuff if you're sitting down.

Bob: Like this isn't the difficult stuff?

Cock: Not yet.

Bob: Great. Okay, first of all, I'm standing here looking at a dancing bug.

Cock: Well, again, I'm hardly jigging. I'm merely standing erect. Isn't that the normal protocol with humans—erect stances?

Bob: It's not polite to interrupt.

Cock: But, I—

Bob: Second of all, you talk. Third of all, it's in a language I can understand. Fourth of all, you seem to know my name. And fifth of all, you say you're from the future.

Cock: The human predilection for stating the obvious is every bit as tedious as it has been reported to be.

Bob: You're interrupting again.

Cock: My apologies.

Bob: As I was saying, here you are—a walking, talking, English-fluent roach named Cock who knows my name and drops by on the day I get fired over the Y2K scandal, and then wants me to come along with him to the future.

Cock: Beautifully reported, Bob.

Bob: You want me to stand here and take all this in and not have my head explode?! What is going on?!

Cock: All right, all right, take it easy. No need to get all bug-eyed, Bob. Just settle down—and sit down—and we'll take this whole thing more slowly from the beginning.

Bob: Much obliged.

Cock: It starts like this: You were right about what you predicted will happen with the Y2K bug.

Bob: Finally, some validation.

Cock: But you don't even know how right you were.

Bob: What do you mean?

Cock: Given the incredible interdependencies among the social, physical, financial, and technological infrastructures you humans created, certain unthinkable and irreversible consequences were realized.

Bob: You have my attention. Go on.

Cock: In addition to the nuclear weapons, the germ warfare weapons, the nuclear reactors, and all the time bomb stockpiles of conventional and chemical weapons all over the world, many more things are going to explode, collapse, and detonate.

Bob: How do you know about my predictions?

Cock: We've studied this era extensively. The archeological evidence is absolutely irrefutable, positively conclusive. It's all much worse than even you can imagine.

Bob: How could it be?! I've already imagined a global catastrophe where about two-thirds of humankind are killed.

Cock: Sadly, for you, it's worse. Far worse.

Bob: But how?

Cock: The global-wide nuclear explosions and detonations will not only devastate in and of themselves, but they will also set off a chain reaction of natural catastrophes that simply cannot be reversed.

Bob: Such as?

Cock: Fireballs, continent-wide forest fires, avalanches, tsunamis, hurricanes, volcanoes, earthquakes, floods, tidal waves—you name it, it happens. Entire continents sink, long-buried continental shelves rise, the polar ice caps melt, the ozone layer shreds, and the very magnetic field that holds the planet together rips, rotating the Earth on its axis, producing, literally, a world upside down. It's a global catastrophe never before witnessed in the planet's multibillion-year history.

Bob: No.

Cock: Yes.

Bob: So much for contingency plans and backup systems.

Cock: And then, over it all, like the last whisper of death, the Sun's rays are blocked by all the debris floating in the air, and a nuclear winter descends upon three-fourths of the Earth's surface, covering all remaining life for many thousands of years.

Bob: No.

Cock: You said that already.

Bob: The end of the world?

Cock: More like the end of an era. Certainly the end of the world as you know it.

Bob: Ah, yes. The End Of The World As We Know It. We've been expecting that.

Cock: Your expectations were duly met. All forms of life that you would recognize—including humans, of course—will cease to exist within a few years. Trees, plants, animals, even Scientologists. All will be wiped from the face of the Earth, with many examples of various species perfectly preserved in the fossil and archeological record for those life-forms that evolve afterwards—many millions of years later, mind you—to discover and ponder over your exotic features.

Bob: Everything gone? Nothing survives?

Cock: Almost nothing. Except us.

Bob: *Cockroaches?!*

Cock: Don't act so surprised, Bob. We're incredible creatures of adaptation. Our genes can mutate from generation to generation to adjust to a hostile environment. Besides, the physical conditions were ripe. After the ice caps melted, every piece of land not completely submerged was extremely moist, just like we like it. And with the ozone ripped, we were one of the few creatures who could withstand the radiation.

Bob: You can withstand rads?

Cock: Rads?

Bob: Radiation Absorbed Dose.

Cock: Of course. Yes, we can withstand "rads" much more than you fragile creatures. Where humans will experience damage at the cellular level when exposed to a mere 300 rads—you will actually die from exposure of anything from 400 to 1,000 rads. But even ordinary domestic cockroaches of your own time could absorb around 10,000 rads before dying. Over time, our species has evolved to endure almost limitless exposures to radiation.

Bob: How nice for you.

Cock: And it's a good thing, too, considering how you blasted most of the ozone off the planet.

Bob: But roaches? It's roaches who inherit the Earth?

Cock: Meet the meek.

Bob: It figures.

Cock: Of course, we inherited it along with certain other tenacious creatures, namely: strains of antibiotic-resistant viruses, various strands of chemotactic bacteria, and a few primitive species of photosynthetic bacteria, what you might call blue-green algae.

Bob: It doesn't make any sense.

Cock: It makes evolutionary sense. All of these species are able to withstand extremely high doses of radiation—we also all share an ability to mutate substantially within one or two generations in order to adapt to radical changes in our environment. Sadly, most species were not so elastic, genetically speaking.

Bob: My condolences all around.

Cock: And, as for cockroaches…well, we've always been precocious. After all, our ancestors were around 350 million years before humans, and we were the earliest insects to evolve wings.

Bob: And when did you evolve into prophets of doom?

Cock: Try not to take it so hard, Bob. It's all part of the cycles of life. Every species, like every civilization, has its rise and fall. You've got to think of the big picture—Mother Earth, the solar system, the galaxy, the universe.

Bob: But it's a picture without any Bobs in it! Just roaches.

Cock: Not even. The species I come from has little in common with, say, your typical German domestic cockroach, the *Blattella germanica*. Only about as much as you have in common with the pond scum from which you eventually evolved.

Bob: No need for evolutionary insults. Let's just stick to straightening this out, okay?

Cock: Sure. Shall we review the chain of events? The Y2K bug will cause widespread nuclear meltdowns and the unleashing of germ warfare stockpiles, among other life-ending horrors, including the collapse of the worldwide power grid.

Bob: And *those* bad things are going to cause even *more* bad things?

Cock: Yes. Specifically, a series of natural disasters such as forest fires, tidal waves, earthquakes, volcanic eruptions, etc., followed by a global nuclear winter. These multiple catastrophes will essentially eliminate life as you know it.

Bob: It's so mind-numbing.

Cock: Actually, it's so simple. It's so beautifully simple, isn't it?

Bob: No. Sometimes when I think about it, when I really think about it, it seems inconceivable that a mere presumption about dates and years in the programming of computers...

Cock: ...could create the seeds to your own utter and complete demise?

Bob: Exactly.

Cock: I understand. It must be hard for you to realize that something so simple could destroy everything you've built here in your complicated, interdependent, computer-run world. But, sadly, Bob, those are the breaks.

Bob: And there's nothing to be done about it?

Cock: Nothing—except to make your peace with your soul.

Bob: It all just sort of snuck up on us.

Cock: Menaces to civilization rarely declare themselves, Bob.

Bob: Will somebody wake me up when this is over?

Cock: Well, Bob, that's just the trouble. It's already over. It's already too late. I'm merely here to offer you an opportunity to live— whereas all others will die.

Bob: You're scaring me.

Cock: Yes, I'm sure it must be frightening. But, Bob, in your deepest, truest marrow you know it already to be true. Your world will end. Your time has come. And not just for you, but for all of your kind and for all of the unfortunate species who are now inextricably tied up with you and your kind.

Bob: Just what are you trying to say?

Cock: I'm not trying to say it, Bob. I've already said it: Your world is finished. Life as you know it on this planet is over. Apocalypse. Armageddon. The Final Hour.

Bob: The Y2K bug will *really* end it all?

Cock: Let's just say it hastened things considerably.

Bob: Humans, civilization, life—gone? All from a stupid programming mistake?

Cock: Oh, Bob, don't get so obsessed with the technical details! It's not like you were going to come out of it alive *anyway*.

Bob: What are you talking about?

Cock: You were a doomed species, Bob. Almost from the beginning. Even without the computer time bomb.

Bob: No hope for humans—even *without* all the computers crashing?! Even without all the bombs exploding and the nuclear reactors crumbling?!

Cock: Yes, Bob, even without all that.

Bob: There was no hope for us anyway?!

Cock: Nope. None whatsoever.

Bob: I can't believe it!

Cock: I'm sorry to have to inform you that you were a failed experiment.

Bob: What?!

Cock: Humans. You were a failed experiment. A lost species, a dead end on the evolutionary map. Why, the more advanced you became—socially and technologically, speaking—the more out of touch you fell from the rhythms of nature. Not to mention your own internal rhythms, too. Even worse, you had no understanding that the rhythms of nature *were* your own rhythms. Separated from this primal fact of life, all you could do was fight for control *over* things instead of working in conjunction *with* things.

Bob: Why are you including me in all this?

Cock: Bob, you are part and parcel of the entire living planet. The daily actions of you and millions—no, *billions*—just like you most certainly contributed to the demise of your own kind, as well as the severe crippling of the planet.

Bob: You're talking about things like the destruction of the rain forests?

Cock: That and a thousand other atrocities just like it.

Bob: But I didn't do that! Not personally.

Cock: Oh, Bob. You humans are so quaint sometimes. Deforestation, holes in the ozone layer, acid rain, oil spills, global warming, the dumping of radioactive waste, man-made viruses—those are just the egregious examples. But just because you didn't personally invent the atomic bomb doesn't mean that you're not responsible for creating and participating in the society that did. Anyway, there are thousands of more subtle examples in your own life that are similar in kind, if not scale.

Bob: Like what?

Cock: Did you ever work late at night?

Bob: Sure. Who didn't? I had lots of important projects—

Cock: Bob. When the Sun goes down, that's your clue to stop working.

Bob: But that's why we invented electricity.

Cock: Electricity is a bad thing.

Bob: We live in a global economy. Nothing stops when the Sun goes down.

Cock: But all life is lived locally. You created global connections and interdependence, but you forgot about local living.

Bob: You're saying the world is going to end because we don't go to sleep when the Sun goes down?

Cock: It's symptomatic, Bob. It's merely one example of a million different things you did wrong—on a mass level. As a result, people who worked at night had higher rates of disease and shorter life spans than those who kept their actions in sync with the daylight.

Bob: Doomed just for punching a third-shift time clock?

Cock: Each body has a clock within it. And it's set in time with the stars—not the CEO. The Godhead is indeed a watchmaker. The clocks are us. You restless folks kept trying to reset them.

Bob: I don't even wear a watch.

Cock: You're in fine company then. None of the best creatures do.

Bob: Great. We're in fine company. Fine soon-to-be-dead company.

Cock: If it's any consolation, Bob, maybe you'll be happy to learn that we've studied your era exhaustively, and we've found your species to be the most interesting.

Bob: I'm so flattered. Why?

Cock: Because the most interesting animals are the ones living the most complicated lives.

Bob: You don't say.

Cock: Yes—the creatures living the most complicated lives have the most problems to solve—and that is endlessly fascinating to observe. In fact, we found you the most fascinating of all the intelligent species on our planet who organized societies.

Bob: There were others?!

Cock: Surely you know that?

Bob: You mean the dolphins?

Cock: Actually, I was thinking about the pine trees. We're most sad about the loss of the pine trees.

Bob: What kind of intelligence did pine trees have?!

Cock: They were a perfectly organized society, forming extensive energy connections among themselves and others. They exhibited an almost flawless balance between the individual and the community.

Bob: What are you talking about?

Cock: I'm sorry. I thought you knew. Why, each individual pine tree had within it ten discernible and unique energy centers, which were distributed in such a way, from the roots to the crown, as to facilitate a continual flow of energy throughout the organism. A pine tree basically represents nature's perfect version of a perpetual motion machine, only here the "motion" was pure energy.

Bob: Trees? Trees were the mythical perpetual motion device?

Cock: When two or more pine trees grew together, these energy channels increased tenfold, forming a huge pulsating beacon of energy flowing up, around, and over everything that was in its path.

Bob: I always kind of liked pine trees.

Cock: Now you know why. Some of our scholars have described them as the highest evolved form of life the planet has ever seen, attributing their elevated spiritual state to the constant open flow of energy, saying it was like being in constant meditation. We're very sorry as a species not to have been able to commune with them. You were lucky to exist during the same geo-historical period as them.

Bob: But what about the dolphins? Tell me about them.

Cock: Why get so fixated on the dolphins, Bob? After all, *every* animal, *every* plant, *every* piece of matter has intelligence in it.

Bob: *Every* piece of matter?

Cock: Yes, because matter is energy and energy is life and life is intelligible. I can't take the whole evening explaining to you the basics about the universe that you don't understand. Others of your own species have tried before and it has gone completely unheeded.

Bob: Like who?

Cock: There were many gurus, yogis, and swamis—the ones who sat in perfect peace under the Bodhi tree—those who discoursed on various aspects of the *Dharma*, but I should think you've never heard of any of them.

Bob: I'm a Western kind of guy, actually.

Cock: So, even a few Westerns got some truths right.

Bob: Such as?

Cock: Einstein for instance. Einstein told you the truth about life in a simple equation, but few of you had the courage to understand what it meant.

Bob: You mean, "$E = mc^2$"?

Cock: Of course. Energy and mass are but different manifestations of the same thing—a thing we call the lifeforce. More technically, the equation states, "The energy of a piece of matter equals the mass of the matter multiplied by the speed of light squared." Any idea what that means?

Bob: That matter can be converted into energy. It's the principle behind the atomic bomb.

Cock: I suppose on a purely "technical" level, you might be able to construe your answer as having the dimmest inkling of truth in it. And, yes, that unfortunate contraption the atom bomb is a crude example of the principle being described. But, no, that's not what Einstein's equation truly *means*.

Bob: Please enlighten me.

Cock: This is the inherent truth, the meaning behind Einstein's scientific shorthand expression of it: Everything that exists— that is, every piece of matter, from an electron to a television to a fern to an asteroid—is alive. Every piece of matter, every thing that has mass, is created from a unique combination of energy—and energy is the stuff of life. Therefore, everything that exists is alive, and as such, everything that exists must be treated with the sovereign respect of life.

Bob: How am I supposed to eat, then?

Cock: As low on the food chain as possible.

Bob: A hearty breakfast of bacteria and sunlight?

Cock: There are, of course, organisms who survive on this, but I hear the concerns beneath your sarcasm. Your duty is to cause as little harm as possible. Grains, fruits and vegetables, and water should do you just fine.

Bob: So, according to you, I can't even swat a mosquito?!

Cock: Technically, it would be better to *will* it away.

Bob: As a rational Western man, you're losing me.

Cock: Energy is the building block of life, Bob. Where there is energy, there is life. And since all matter is a form of energy, then all matter is a form of life. I really can't say it any simpler. Except to say $E = mc^2$. But as elegant as that formulation is, I personally think it leaves out much of the philosophical poetry of its truth.

Bob: I'll be sure to put that under advisement.

Cock: While you're at it, you might also contemplate your species' realized capacity for self-destruction, the oneness of all life, the human rape of nature, and the emptiness of your momentary "victories" over the natural world.

Bob: All in good time. But first let's get back to that other interesting point you made—about how humans were the most fascinating of all intelligent species.

Cock: Of course, Narcissus. Can you guess *why* humans are the most interesting of all the intelligent species on the planet who organized societies?

Bob: I'll bite—why?

Cock: Because of the contradictions! Because of the incredible battle that existed between your contradictory impulses! We marvel at the incredible expression of impulses toward life and beauty that existed concurrently with the equally strong and devastating expression of the impulses toward death and destruction.

Bob: The constant struggle between death and life. Freud called it "Thanatos" and "Eros."

Cock: And we call you "The Species That Was and Was Not." In brief, you were heartbreaking, maddening, insufferable, and—now that you're safely gone—endlessly fascinating.

Bob: But what makes us a more fascinating species than say a society of ants or bees?

Cock: We think it may have had something to do with your sense of an independent consciousness, a distinct formulation of an "I" that is somehow separated from nature, from the All That Is. Or perhaps it was your ability to produce a written language. Of course, there was also your disproportionate balance between head intelligence and heart intelligence, and the fact that you were even able to separate the two from each other at all. We're still not sure how you did that.

Bob: "I think, therefore I am." That's how we did it. Well, that's how Descartes did it and the rest of us followed.

Cock: Yes, the Cartesian fallacy set back your spiritual development considerably.

Bob: How so?

Cock: The so-called mind-body split is nothing but a compartmentalization of aspects that can't, or at least shouldn't, be compartmentalized. Moreover, it doesn't even address all aspects of being.

Bob: What's missing?

Cock: The spirit, of course. The mind, the body, and the spirit are all inextricable from each other. In fact, they are just different names, or different aspects, of the same thing—being alive, the lifeforce.

Bob: Ah, yes, being alive—that exquisite, but excruciating, pleasure. Pardon me while I wax poetic: Life, the difficult pleasure.

Cock: The conception of life as composed of three inseparable parts was common enough even in your own species. For the Mayans, the notion of Mind-Body-Spirit was thought of in terms of Man, Nature, and the Gods—and their cosmic view of life held these sacred aspects as inseparable. Likewise, the Christians transformed the threesome into Father, Son, and Holy Ghost, another example of one-in-three cosmology—albeit not as sophisticated or as accurate as the Mayan conception. But, again, the important thing is to realize that all three aspects are involved in the makeup of that thing called existence, and that all three aspects are inseparable from one another.

Bob: That's lovely. Touching, really. But you can't prove it.

Cock: Proof is not what you humans needed. A gargantuan infusion of enlightenment and reconnection to the essence of your own existence was a little more in order.

Bob: But back to Descartes—

Cock: In the first place, the Cartesian fallacy doesn't even acknowledge spirit in its dualistic dissection of the world. And secondly, the Cartesian fallacy separates the remaining two components, which are in fact inseparable. It's simply shocking. All around.

Bob: So this being alive—mind, body, spirit—it's a packaged deal, you say?

Cock: Quite.

Bob: Just like when you go antiquing—never break up a set?

Cock: In a sense. But, even more than concepts such as the Cartesian fallacy, we were fascinated by your species' collective inability to understand your place in the world of nature.

Bob: Isn't our place "in the world of nature" at the pinnacle of evolution? All the earthly delights at our beck and call?

Cock: Yes, you wanted to believe, or were falsely led to believe, that nature was at your disposal, that it was little more than an endless supply of resources from which you could extract the things you desired: oil, coal, iron, lumber, water, air, fruit, fish, game, and gold.

Bob: Well, except for a flood here, a drought there—or an occasional hurricane or earthquake, now that you mention it—we pretty much *do* control things. We pride ourselves, you know, on being masters of our own domain.

Cock: Well, that's just the problem. You had a severe misconception regarding your "domain." What your species didn't understand is that it was just a part of the larger living system of the planet itself. The planet *in toto* is a lifeforce, an organism—and your species, like all species, was merely a smaller component of that larger system.

Bob: I've heard of that theory.

Cock: It's hardly what we would call a "theory." It's the way things are.

Bob: "Gaia," I think it's called. I always thought that was a stupid name for it. How are you going to get a bunch of burly scientists behind a theory if you go and call it "Gaia"? People have no understanding of the nature of science…or names.

Cock: And your species had no understanding of the nature of the planet—whatever you wish to call it.

Bob: What about the "Planet Unification Theory"? Or PUT. That's better, I think. More scientific sounding, definitely.

Cock: As you can see now, with the entire demise of your species, and the triumphant continuation of the life of the planet—

Bob: You're supposed to be proof of that?

Cock: —maybe you can comprehend that the important thing is for the *planet* to survive, not for this or that particular species to survive. When you became too destructive, when your species threatened the very life of the larger system that gave it life, then you quite naturally and understandably had to be terminated.

Bob: Terminated? By who?!

Cock: Why, by the larger system, of course.

Bob: You're saying the Earth itself destroyed us?!

Cock: It's actually more complicated than that. But you could look at it that way. In any event, I'm saying that, out of necessity, and by the dint of evolutionary forces, you ceased to exist as a species.

Bob: What exactly are you saying?

Cock: Basically, you destroyed yourselves for the good of the planet.

Bob: Impossible!

Cock: It's true. Deep within your genetic makeup was the imperative —a genetic imperative, by the way, that you shared with every other species on the planet, past and present—that should you ever be a threat to the greater life of the planet itself, you will self-destruct.

Bob: No.

Cock: Yes. It is a simple safety mechanism built into every species. If a species loses sight of its place within the larger system and starts to threaten the very existence of the larger system—as humans were doing with the Earth—then the species self-destructs in order to save the integrity of the larger system and to preserve it.

Bob: We're going to self-destruct because we're destroying the Earth?

Cock: Yes. Just like the dinosaurs.

Bob: Wait a minute! The dinosaurs didn't "self-destruct." They were wiped out by a huge asteroid from outer space. It had nothing to do with what you're suggesting!

Cock: Oh, Bob. So wedded to the face value of things. Listen, if a species that is threatening the greater system doesn't self-destruct, then it gets a little help from an even larger system.

Bob: It was a random astronomical event!

Cock: There are no random events.

Bob: Are you saying that all of life is predetermined?

Cock: Not determined. Just meaningful. Full of meaning. Nothing is random, but nothing is predestined, either.

Bob: What's the difference?

Cock: There's a Sufi saying that it is not given to humans to know the dividing line between free will and destiny. You are to work your lives out as best you can realizing that there are patterns that go beyond your understanding.

Bob: This does not inspire confidence. What kind of patterns?!

Cock: Bob, have you ever heard of the Butterfly Effect?

Bob: Yes. I've explored some chaos theory.

Cock: It's not about chaos. It's about interconnection. Interconnection, to the untrained eye, merely *appears* to be chaos.

Bob: There's no such thing as chaos? As entropy? But what about the second law of thermodynamics?

Cock: What about it? It's superseded by the penultimate law of thermo-dynamics—increasing organization and intelligence on a high systems level.

Bob: But the laws of physics say—and the second law of thermo-dynamics specifically says—that, in a closed system, information devolves into a more and more disorganized state.

Cock: In certain local, closed systems, yes. But the universe as a whole is not a closed system. A series of interconnected, infinite systems—by definition—cannot be closed.

Bob: I think, therefore I'm getting a thermodynamic headache.

Cock: Look, Bob, not only are you simply a piece of the larger system called the planet, but the planet itself is simply a piece of the larger system called the solar system.

Bob: Oh, please stop.

Cock: I can't—because it doesn't stop even there. You are to the planet as the planet is to the solar system. And the planet is to the solar system as the solar system is to the galaxy. And the solar system...

Bob: Yeah, yeah. And the solar system is to the galaxy as the galaxy is to the universe. Right?

Cock: Well, technically, the galaxies band together forming clusters and those clusters in turn band together forming superclusters. It never ends. Every thing is a piece of a bigger thing, and that bigger thing is but a piece of yet another bigger thing. That is the meaning of infinity.

Bob: All right, Mr. Set of Nesting Dolls. What does this nonsense have to do with the dinosaurs?!

Cock: The dinosaurs were in danger of killing the planet. They had grown too large, too massive. Their physical size was huge, yet their brains were, relatively speaking, small, and their souls were utterly minuscule. On a purely physical level, the amount of food they consumed, just to survive, was enormous. They were eating all the plant life and vegetation. The plants couldn't reproduce fast enough to maintain a sustainable population for themselves and other species, in addition to the dinosaurs, that depended on them.

Bob: You're saying the dinosaurs were literally eating us out of house and home?

Cock: In a manner of speaking, yes. They were seriously disrupting the balance of resources. And, most importantly, they gave nothing back to the cycle of life—except massive amounts of waste.

Bob: What kind of waste?

Cock: Huge piles of toxic excrement expelled via powerful methane gases.

Bob: Like über-cow patties?

Cock: Indeed. As the different dinosaur populations grew, the vegetation populations diminished. It threw off the balance of oxygen and carbon dioxide in the air, as well as the level of methane. A greenhouse effect mushroomed into being practically overnight by geological standards, raising temperatures and melting the polar ice caps. By all rights, the dinosaurs should have died out. That would have put things back in balance. But they didn't. Instead, they began to proliferate. Somehow, something went terribly wrong—their genetic imperative, the planetary safety mechanism, didn't work.

Bob: Their genetic self-destruct button didn't kick in?

Cock: Exactly. But the puzzling bit is that, so far, we can't tell if it was on purpose or not.

Bob: Hello?! What are you saying?

Cock: The dinosaurs may have willed their own genetic makeup to ignore the genetic imperative to self-destruct.

Bob: I don't believe what I'm hearing.

Cock: Why not? The power of thought and will is every bit as potent as physical action. Besides, humans currently can mechanically manipulate their own genetic materials, going so far as to be able to clone human cells, and to isolate stem cells. Do you think you're the only species to have a working knowledge of the processes of life? Or an understanding of deoxyribonucleic acid? Again, how quaint. And how utterly inaccurate.

Bob: But dinosaurs…I thought they were just big, terrible lizards!

Cock: Hardly. Did you know that they gathered in great flocks on the plains of Argentina, from all over the world, in annual Sun-worshipping pilgrimages to lay eggs?

Bob: Surprisingly, Mr. Cock, no—that was one bit of history of which I was not aware.

Cock: It all took place at a vast nesting site in northwest Patagonia. Moreover, they laid their eggs in huge circular patterns that formed a type of calendar.

Bob: A calendar?!

Cock: Yes. And even more interesting, we found that those egg-laid calendars were very similar to the astronomical markings of certain Mayan calendars.

Bob: Truly amazing, Mr. Wizard.

Cock: But wait, there's more. From the egg calendars they left, we know that the dinosaurs understood the mathematical concept of zero.

Bob: I don't even know what to say.

Cock: So, you see, this dinosaur species was much more complicated than your human species ever realized.

Bob: Yet another piece of science I have neglected to understand.

Cock: Thus, it's no wonder you can't imagine dinosaurs as being capable of willing their own genetic code to override the self-destruct imperative. But some of our most respected scholars believe they did exactly that. Other scholars, of course, think it was less conscious, a more natural mutation—some bizarre freak of nature. But, either way, before the death of the planet became irreversible, the asteroid arrived—right on schedule, near the Yucatan, 65 million years ago—drastically altering weather patterns worldwide, plummeting the world into darkness and cold, killing off the heinous dinosaurs, and setting the balance of nature right again.

Bob: Okay, let me get this straight. The asteroid that killed the dinosaurs—dinosaurs that, by the way, you claim understood zero, worshipped the Sun, and laid eggs in a pattern that served as calendars!—this asteroid was an intended Act of God? An outer-space, special assignment assassin?

Cock: More or less. Those are the broad outlines to the story. Though it's all much more complicated than I could possibly take the time to explain right now.

Bob: Well, sure. Save it for the next time you come around. And don't wait so long to visit while you're at it.

Cock: Of course, it was the eradication of the dinosaurs that set the stage for the development and rise of the smaller class of animals known as mammals—and that's where you humans come in and, sadly, where history begins to repeat itself. That's really the topic at hand, Bob.

Bob: Yes, indeed. So, let's get back to talking about my terrible tribe, and not those "heinous" dinosaurs.

Cock: All other species find it to their benefit to survive and thrive within the balance of nature, taking and giving in equal proportions. Your species—like the dinosaurs, mind you—got stuck on taking.

Bob: So we're back to your previous contention—that humans depleted the resources of the Earth and the Earth struck back.

Cock: Don't blame the Earth, Bob. You don't blame your own immune system for eliminating a virus, do you?

Bob: A virus? Now we're a virus? Do your insults know no bounds?

Cock: Excuse me. You're right. I'm sorry. Not like a virus.

Bob: Thank you.

Cock: More like a cancer.

Bob: A cancer?!

Cock: Yes. The human species was a cancer on the planet.

Bob: Oh, please...

Cock: The human race was a kind of self-destructive cancer. Even some of your own kind knew it to be true.

Bob: Like who?

Cock: Perhaps Malthus was the first, with his theories on exponential population growth and the limits of the planetary carrying capacity, but even in your own time there were many others. Doctors James Lovelock and Lynn Margulis were the first visionaries to postulate the underlying science of it in their Gaia work. And then, for instance, you can take a certain Dr. Warren Hern, an epidemiologist who noted that satellite photographs of urban centers taken over a period of years showed a striking similarity to images of cancer invading healthy surrounding tissue.

Bob: Are you serious?

Cock: Deadly. Dr. Hern also noted that in many instances human population was rapid and uncontrolled; that it invaded and destroyed natural habitats; that in so doing, it killed off many species and thus reduced the differentiation of nature. All these features are likewise characteristic of cancerous tumors.

Bob: Where did you come up with all that?

Cock: Well, the theory is absolutely correct—not only does it make intuitive sense, but our archeological studies have confirmed it —but we read about your species' discovery of this truth in a book called *THE NEW YORK TIMES, TUESDAY, DECEMBER 22, 1998.* It was written by someone called Malcolm Browne.

Bob: Indeed. Too bad for me I didn't read that book. You know, for me, it's still only September.

Cock: Too bad for your species that those who did read it didn't heed it.

Bob: So this is what you have to say to me—that the human race is a self-destructive cancer and a blight to the planet?

Cock: Yes. A cancer that finally, and appropriately for the good of the planet, excised itself.

Bob: Sounds terribly masochistic to me.

Cock: Think of it more as a necessary sacrifice your species finally made for the good of the larger system. After all, your annihilation made it possible for the planet to continue to survive and—eventually, after millions of years of repair work—thrive.

Bob: You'll pardon me if I don't stand up and cheer.

Cock: The other bright side is that without your complete demise and the geophysical aftermath you caused with your exploding contraptions, our species never could have evolved to our status as the primary intelligent life force that it is now.

Bob: You're so very welcome.

Cock: And, of course, by studying you so closely—we're as fascinated with you as you were with the dinosaurs—we were able to learn from your mistakes and have been loathe to repeat them.

Bob: What mistakes?!

Cock: Isn't it obvious, Bob? This is what makes your species so fascinating: You placed yourself outside the natural order of things. Somehow in your development—was it tools? was it language? was it war? was it an ego-based consciousness?—you placed yourselves above and beyond the balance of nature. You operated on the inaccurate view of yourselves as separate, autonomous beings independent of the web of life all around you, and from which you sprang.

Bob: Was nobody worth saving?

Cock: Oh sure, there were some of your species that approximated living in balance with nature, that understood the inherent interconnectedness of all things, but they were eventually killed off or subjugated by the other humans, the humans who came to define what your species would be.

Bob: Just what was it that was so wrong with us?

Cock: Your greatest strength was also your greatest weakness. And it was this dual-edged sword that led to your ultimate, complete, and inevitable demise.

Bob: But what was it?!

Cock: You had the ability—a monstrous ability—to ignore the sovereignty of other living things.

Bob: Oh, that.

Cock: You had the ability—a monstrous ability—to marshal all the resources of the Earth, including even members of your own species, to meet your own myopic ends.

Bob: I thought it was supposed to be about survival of the fittest?

Cock: Certainly not to the detriment of all other living things. And remember, all things are living things. That's survival of the foolish. And only a temporary survival at that.

Bob: Surely we weren't born bad?

Cock: Of course not. You came from all that came before you. In fact, each human, like each organism, lives in a body that is itself an archive of all that has come before it. We are all museums of life. Humans, like all organisms, evolved from the goodness that is the Earth. You certainly had the potential to turn out differently. It's just that the choices you made led you down deep, irrecoverable paths.

Bob: Where did it all start?

Cock: Innocently enough, we think. First it was the grain. You learned to plant and harvest. That meant you had a stable food supply and could support a larger population. It also gave you the sense that you could and did exert enormous control over your environment—and that sense of control, much to your detriment, elevated your collective egos.

Bob: A kinder, gentler cockroach would call it "self-confidence."

Cock: Then it was the animals. You domesticated them and they became your work tools—suddenly you could physically accomplish much more than you ever dreamed possible. It wasn't long before some of you tried it with other humans. They became your slaves and built your pyramids, your great walls, your aqueducts, and your skyscrapers.

Bob: Talk about your slippery-slope—from corn to conglomerates.

Cock: Of course, you didn't stop there. It wasn't enough to control and denigrate other humans—you went on to desecrate the entire natural environment. You bulldozed the forests, polluted the rivers and oceans, poked holes in the sky, pumped chemicals into the livestock, and covered the land in garbage and concrete all to create your economies and transport your goods, to accumulate your riches and maintain your kingly standards of living. The sky, the water, the land, the animals, the vegetation, the children, the slaves, the poor—all became objects in your ever-growing quest for domination. You had an insatiable lust for power, for wealth, for opulent comforts, for control.

Bob: In case you're interested, not much of that opulence actually came my way.

Cock: And all the while, you ignored the beating of your own heart, the steady rhythm that told you peace and harmony were within and could be secured through a communal relationship with all things great and small. You created the gilded edifice and architecture of the outside, while inward, in the small, still part of your soul, the abyss widened. Eventually, your connections to the eternal rhythms of nature were completely sundered.

Nothing you could throw into this abyss from the outside could fill its bottomless depths—not all the money, all the wealth, all the power, all the fame, all the glory, all the food, all the wine, all the sex, all the sugar, all the song. None of it. For the soul thrives in the harmony of the life around it. And your species had disrupted—to monstrous proportions—the harmony of all life around you.

Bob: This doesn't sound like it's going to turn out well.

Cock: The climate changed, the Earth warmed, the ocean belched back onto its shores the dung you had dumped into it—and, yet, you heeded it not. Still you buried your radioactive waste in the belly of the Earth, still you dumped toxins into the rivers, still you massacred those whose beliefs or bones were different than your own. The rivers turned to blood, the sky to soot, and the fields to ashes. And still you heard not the small, still voice that said, "Enough, no more."

Bob: Not exactly the kind of species you'd want to bring home to mother, huh?

Cock: Not even a nice place to visit.

Bob: Ouch.

Cock: You created so much. And yet you had so little.

Bob: Humans…the lonely species.

Cock: No, not alone. Just a loner.

Bob: And now a goner.

Cock: No—now gone.

Bob: You know…just how do you know so much about us anyway? Did you watch all the PBS specials in the Library of Congress?

Cock: Books and some static images were all that survived, Bob. That and a few examples of architecture. But mostly it was the words, pictograms, ideographs preserved on paper, stone tablets, inscriptions on buildings. The other media and mediums are too dependent on attendant devices for recording and playback.

Bob: What do you mean?

Cock: I mean, we have dozens of scripts, but not one movie. We have dozens of manuals, but not one computer. We have dozens of liner notes, but not one recording.

Bob: No movies? No music?

Cock: It's always the words that survive—the handprint on a cave wall, the clay tablet, the *Book of Kells*, a Gideon *Bible*. Human history alone should have taught you that.

Bob: Not one video? Not one CD?

Cock: Ephemeral media, Bob. Recorded sounds and visuals are always of the moment. Sure, they can be preserved for decades, sometimes even a century, but not much longer than that. History corrupts it. Time destroys it. Even if the nitrate in film, or the silicon in video, didn't decompose over time, can you image the film projector or VCR that would still be working in a thousand years? Impossible. You know, if you want something to last a million years or more, you better fossilize it. The Egyptians had the right idea—carve it in stone.

Bob: So I guess you've never heard of the Beatles?

Cock: Are you making a pun, Bob? Yes, I know who the Beatles were —but more importantly I know who they were to you and your culture. I have read descriptions of their music and the effect their music had on others. I have seen the lyrics to their songs and even the notations on some extremely rare fragments of sheet music. But, no, I have not heard their sounds—anymore than you have heard the sounds of a medieval Celtic troupe. You have scholars and performers who try their best to approximate the sounds and even play them on recreated instruments which are, hopefully, somewhat faithful to the period. But no one in your culture really knew what a 12th-century band of musicians sounded like.

Bob: I'm starting to feel a little melancholy.

Cock: Perhaps the passing of time itself is sad to you. That certainly seems to be the rampaging sentiment among you humans. But you could view it another way—that that is the integrity of each age: to keep its secrets. To enjoy some unique moment never to be repeated or seen again in exactly the same way in the history of the universe. That is the pulse of life, of living. That is the ecstasy of the present.

Bob: Just what is so "ecstatic" about time passing and destroying everything in its wake?

Cock: Precisely this: that this exact moment will never again exist in exactly the same way. Therefore, this moment is to be cherished as the unique, precious instant it is. And all of life is nothing more than a never-ending succession of just such exquisite moments. That's what your species was never quite able to grasp—on a mass level. Of course, some individuals of your collective intuitively understood it. A few of them formed like-minded societies and communes, passing these beliefs on to disciples or children. But very few were ever actually able to live with this heady knowledge of the Exquisite Nature of the Present Moment, day after day, year after year.

Bob: But your so-called "present moment" is nothing but a piece of nothingness, instantaneously obliterated by a past which is already gone and a future which has yet to arrive.

Cock: No, my time-weary friend. The present is a moment of such fullness, of such presence that to experience it fully is very much like to die and be born again simultaneously and continuously, rapturously without end. Eternity itself is contained within the present, a moment of utter presence and complete timelessness, to which there can never be an adequately worded description.

Bob: But it's too hard to—

Cock: Precisely because your species could not hold onto the present, humans developed an obsession for preserving and documenting the past. From our perspective, we view this tendency as a sickness—a disease, if you will. A time-sickness. Whatever it was, it surely was unnatural and not part of the spontaneous process of living.

Bob: But how do we hold on to things—precious things, things we care about—if we don't record them and preserve them?

Cock: Nothing that exists is ever lost, Bob. All life, all sounds, all knowledge, all dreams, all wisdom, all love live on forever in the mind of the Godhead.

Bob: That god-damned "head" is giving me a headache.

Cock: We are all part of that Godhead, and each of us contribute to the collective memory, the collective consciousness, the collective lifeforce that is the sum total of All That Is.

Bob: Are you sure you came from the future...and not some huge bong party, circa 1967 maybe?

Cock: "O ye of little faith. The truth hath been spoken and, like children wandering in the darkness, you understand and heareth it not."

Bob: Cheery chap, aren't you?

Cock: That's a quote, Bob. I studied up before I came here. So I could say things that might be familiar to you and help to put you at ease. How's it working?

Bob: Like a charm. Like a fucking lucky charm.

Cock: Then I'm pleased. Very pleased.

Bob: All right, let me ask you something. If all you say is true—that humans are a failed experiment and that we're going to destroy the Earth with our little Y2K problem—and that even if we don't, if somehow we manage to fix the computer problem, in the long run it won't matter because we're a doomed, lost, hideously unevolved species anyway—if all this is true, if you're from the future and my people are toast, then *WHY ARE YOU HERE TELLING ME THIS?* Is it just to torture me—with all of this hideous awareness?

Cock: Like I said at the very outset, Bob: I've come here today to ask you to return with me to the future. Well—strictly speaking—your future, my present.

Bob: But if you're so advanced, what could you possibly want from us?

Cock: Not "us," Bob. You.

Bob: Me? There's something special about me?

Cock: As hard as it was for us to believe it initially—yes. The irrefutable answer seems to be: there's something about Bob.

Bob: How you flatter me—please go on.

Cock: There is a great mystery in our culture that baffles us to no end. And all the evidence leads to you as the human who can help us decipher it.

Bob: Me? Why me?

Cock: Sometimes the truth has been shown to a person or a group of persons who themselves don't understand the profundity of what they've seen. That seems to have been the case with your species, in general, and with you, in particular.

Bob: Could you be a little more specific?

Cock: Well, frankly, we were quite surprised when we finally discovered that yours was a Sun-worshipping culture.

Bob: A what?!

Cock: A Sun-worshipping culture. We were surprised to find that you were a society of Sun worshippers.

Bob: For your information, Cock Meister, no one in Western industrial society is a Sun worshipper. Oh, maybe a pocket of nutbags here and there—a trailer park in Napa Valley, a commune in Spokane—but nothing serious enough to register on the cultural radar screen. It looks like you made your little trip for nothing.

Cock: But *all* the great civilizations were Sun worshippers.

Bob: Well, we aren't.

Cock: Precisely. That was the missing link. We couldn't understand how your culture could have attained the level of sophistication you did *without* being Sun worshippers. On the other hand, because you were so morally and spiritually bankrupt, we couldn't imagine how you *could* be Sun worshippers either. You didn't seem to have the necessary reverence for nature and the natural realm that Sun worshipping implies. It's been a tremendous mystery for generations.

Bob: Insults aside, your theory is off. Believe me, except for a few rollerbladers on Venice Beach, nobody is a Sun worshipper.

Cock: "Give to me the splendid silent Sun, with all his beams full dazzling." What about that?

Bob: Another quote?

Cock: By a Walt Whitman.

Bob: To make me feel at ease, no doubt.

Cock: Do you deny the unassailable truth of the life-giving gifts of the almighty Sol?

Bob: Look, sure the Sun is important, but it—

Cock: "Important"?! Is that all you have to say about it?

Bob: Well, I mean—

Cock: "Important." That's what I would call "putting it mildly." We are all here because the Sun was here before us. Shining steadily, brightly, consistently, for billions of years. We exist because the Sun exists. And we will continue to exist because this churning, life-sustaining sphere of energy grants us light and thus life. When the Sun dies, we die. While it lives, we live. So, as you can see, Bob, it's a little more than, as you say, "important."

Bob: I can see you have feelings about this, but it's really never been an object of…worship for me.

Cock: Then you haven't given it enough thought.

Bob: Well, then, in your opinion, just what should the Sun mean to me?

Cock: That's not up to me or anyone else to decide. However, the important thing is that the Sun mean *something* to you. The important thing is that it have some meaning to you. Otherwise, you are so divorced from your essence and your creation that nothing can save you. Which was, as we've seen, exactly the case.

Bob: This is all very enlightening, if you'll pardon the pun. But you're not listening to me—nobody in our society is a Sun worshipper!

Cock: No, you're wrong. Because we found it. Concrete archeological evidence—

Bob: Well, as long as it was concrete…

Cock: —leading us to The Great Temple of the Sun's Arc. We found the irrefutable, undeniable physical evidence of your primary religion—and, indeed, it was based on worshipping the cycles of the Sun.

Bob: I don't understand.

Cock: Bob, we're confused, too. Not just because you, in fact, turned out to be Sun worshippers, but because there seems to be an even greater truth hidden in the Temple. A truth so big and so grand that we cannot even begin to comprehend it.

Bob: What do you mean?

Cock: There are *two* Suns being worshipped. The Great Temple of the Arc specifically delineates *two* Suns as being worshipped, with two distinct trajectories plotted.

Bob: Are you sure you landed in the correct solar system?

Cock: Positively. Your Earth today is the very Earth of our distant past. And our greatest thinkers have pondered, postulated, and pontificated on the meaning of the Second Sun. It is one of the last great mysteries to be solved about your society and our planetary system. We are full of questions.

Bob: That makes two of us.

Cock: Were the cataclysmic events that ushered in the Winter of a Thousand Years—

Bob: The Y2K explosions?

Cock: Certainly some kind of "explosions"…cataclysmic in nature. Were these the events responsible for the disappearance of the Second Sun? Or did you humans—out of jealously, out of hatred, out of ignorance—destroy the Second Sun? Use it up for fuel? If so, how? Why? Most importantly, where did the Second Sun go, and why are there no cosmic traces left of it? What was its original purpose? How has the balance of nature been disrupted with its disappearance? Is it irrecoverable or is there something we can do in order to set the balance right again? You see, Bob, we are desperate for answers to one of the greatest mysteries of our age.

Bob: Gee, I feel your pain. You know, I'm a former philosophy major and all—in fact, I was a double major with computer science— so I can appreciate, really I can, all your gargantuan cockroach angst about this. But really, really dear little horror figment of my imagination…WHAT DOES THIS ALL HAVE TO DO WITH ME?! WHY ARE YOU TORTURING ME WITH YOUR UNGODLY VISITATION?!

Cock: Isn't it obvious to you by now?! Do you think I made this horrid journey back here to this wretched civilization just for my health?! Just to anoint you with the burden that your world, your civilization is on the brink of permanent destruction? Do you think I risked my one life and six limbs to give you a tepid little Halloween scare?! I think not, Bob. I think not.

Bob: Hey, you never know.

Cock: Bob, *you* hold the knowledge we seek! *You* are the key to the mystery of The Great Temple of the Sun's Arc. *You* are the answer to the vexing question of the Second Sun.

Bob: Really, I think you've confused me with Indiana Jones.

Cock: No, no—I'm sure of the coordinates—it distinctly said "Minnesota Bob." You are the Bob we seek. You are the Bob among Bobs.

Bob: ARGGGH! I can't stand this anymore! Why don't I just kill myself right now!

Cock: Really, Bob, just because your world is going to end, don't let it ruin your life.

Bob: Spoken like a true insect. Do you things even have mothers?

Cock: Everything has a past, Bob. But just because you're scared is no reason to be rude.

Bob: I could squash you like a bug.

Cock: Of course you could. We've not precluded that possibility. We made the decision a long time ago to deal with you on your own terms—as violent and fear-based as that might be—because we need your full cooperation in order to transport you back into our time.

Bob: Why? Why not just take me by force? If you can pop in and out of my house, surely you can drag me along helter-skelter into the future.

Cock: Even if it were possible—and physically it's not—we wouldn't do it that way. It's not our nature to force things. Therefore, we've decided to risk your native impulses, as ugly and unpredictable as they might be.

Bob: You're sure not helping your cause by calling me names. It just makes me want to squish you even more.

Cock: I'm fully prepared to die during this mission.

Bob: I'll be sure to send a telegram to the missus.

Cock: Of course, if that happens—if I die or if you kill me—we will simply send another, and another, and another, until you realize that we are sincere in our mission and tenacious in our request, until you realize that we wish you no harm and that you have nothing to fear from us. On the other hand, you absolutely may opt to die here with your species—certainly that is your choice, and it would have been your natural fate had we not discovered your historical importance.

Bob: Are you sure I'll die if I stay?

Cock: It's an absolute mathematical certainty. All humans die within a decade or so of the global catastrophes. We've found the archeological record of it all. And believe me, Bob, five billion humans all dying within a few years of each other is not a pretty sight.

Bob: *Everyone* dies?

Cock: I know it's hard to fathom, but that is the fate of all humans and most other life-forms on this planet at your current historical moment. However, you alone, Bob, have a unique decision to make—you may die with your kind, as you were meant to, or you may choose to live and come back to the future with me, as part of an intellectual expedition, helping our species better understand yours and thereby understanding a little better our own evolutionary history.

Bob: If I go back with you, am I going to end up in some bubbling cauldron?

Cock: Beg your pardon?

Bob: Are you going to eat me?!

Cock: No, Bob, I won't be eating you. Like the rest of my species, I'm a vegetarian. And, for your added peace of mind, please try to remember that we've been vegetarians—and I mean *real* vegetarians, not the "I only eat chicken, fish, and Bobs" vegetarians—for millions and millions of years.

Bob: What about me? Is there anything I can eat where you come from?

Cock: I'm quite confident that our food staples will provide you with an adequate supply of nutrients to live out your natural life span.

Bob: Okay, so say I decide to go—what do I have to do?

Cock: Well, the first thing you have to do is merely agree to come back with me. Most of all, I need your willful intent and cooperation. But you must provide these immediately. The Sun will be coming up soon and I don't have much time left.

Bob: What do you mean?

Cock: Time travel is an extremely difficult and extremely dangerous enterprise, Bob. There are finite windows of opportunity through which we can enter and leave a specific spacetime coordinate.

Bob: Why?

Cock: It has to do with the amazingly complex structure of the spacetime continuum and how eternity is present in every moment—something I alluded to earlier.

Bob: I told you I was a philosophy major. I did my senior thesis on the nature of time. I'd be very interested to have you explain it all to me.

Cock: I'm sorry, Bob. I can't—maybe later when we arrive. Spacetime is undeniably the deepest of all mysteries in physics. But right now, we're running out of it.

Bob: I won't go back with you unless you explain it to me.

Cock: This seems to be an example of a human being manipulative.

Bob: Cut the commentary. Just spill the beans.

Cock: Okay. When objects go backward in time, they behave some-what differently from when they move forward through time.

Bob: Help me out here.

Cock: For instance, when I travel back in time—from the perspective of my point of origin—it takes me more actual moments than when I travel forward in time to return to my point of origin.

Bob: That seems odd. Why?

Cock: It has to do with a principle understood even in your world—the conservation of the C.P.T. components of matter.

Bob: C.P.T.?

Cock: The Charge, Parity, and Time of particles on a quantum level. Complicated physics aside, the upshot is: To move backward in time is a slower process than to move forward in time.

Bob: Kind of like catching a tailwind—or fighting against one?

Cock: Precisely. To move backward in time, a body has to go against the natural forward thrust of time already built into the workings of the universe. And vice versa—so that when a body moves forward in time, the built-in forward thrust of natural time accelerates the process.

Bob: I see.

Cock: Probably not.

Bob: Why not?

Cock: Because this phenomenon is only one of the many variables of spacetime travel.

Bob: What are others?

Cock: Another is that I must reappear at my point of origin at the *precise instant* in which I left. Thus, from my point of origin, it would seem as if I hadn't been gone at all.

Bob: That sounds difficult to pull off.

Cock: Believe me, it is.

Bob: But why is that important?

Cock: Because I must have a continuity of existence in my world of origin. If I come back *before* the time that I departed, then I'll have a double existence—which is not only inconvenient, but physically impossible. On the other hand, if I come back *after* the time that I departed, then for some period of time in the world of my point of origin I will not have existed—which is equally inconvenient and likewise physically impossible. In other words, either condition results in the physical annihilation of the traveler.

Bob: In a word—dead?

Cock: In four words—deader than a doorknob.

Bob: But what about me? What happens to me if I suddenly pop into your world?

Cock: Nothing. You didn't exist there at all before, and now you do. It's like a birth. But in this case, you spring forth fully formed.

Bob: I kind of like that idea. But how do you coordinate all this precise entrancing and exiting?

Cock: Please, Bob, I don't have time to explain any more of it. Let it suffice to say that spacetime travel is an extremely tricky business and I have to be out of here, with or without you, before the Sun comes up, or my Mother of All Gooses is forever cooked. That's the situation. Now decide: Yes or no.

Bob: Just like that—yes or no?

Cock: I'm sorry, but that's how it is. You got me sidetracked on a lot of different subjects I hadn't intended to go into and now we're out of time.

Bob: Can't I even make some phone calls and say good-bye?

Cock: Absolutely not.

Bob: Why not?

Cock: First of all, we don't have time. And second of all, your friends and family wouldn't understand your leaving and you'd find yourself capitulating to sentiment.

Bob: Yeah, I hate it when I do that.

Cock: Again, we're out of time. Decide.

Bob: I can't.

Cock: You have to tell me *now*.

Bob: I can't.

Cook: You must.

Bob: I'm thinking!

Cock: Oh, well, then—since you're *thinking*—there's one other thing I forgot to mention.

Bob: Now what?

Cock: If you come back with me, you won't be able to return.

Bob: You mean I'm stuck in your world, no matter what?

Cock: Precisely.

Bob: But why?

Cock: Well, first of all, you can't return to your own time because, basically, your world is going to end. Even if we could send you back after the nuclear catastrophes were over, it's impossible to say what you would die of first: lack of heat, starvation, radiation poisoning, or loneliness.

Bob: Well, except for the radiation, you basically described my typical Saturday night.

Cock: But most importantly, you won't be able to return to this time— or any other—because of the nature of spacetime travel itself.

Bob: What do you mean?

Cock: Spacetime travel is extremely strenuous on material objects—especially complicated ones like sentient beings. And even though you will, in all likelihood, survive spacetime travel in one direction, you certainly wouldn't be able to survive a return trip.

Bob: Why not?

Cock: It's just too much wear and tear on your quanta.

Bob: My what?

Cock: Your quanta...as in quantum physics. Quanta are the discrete packets of energy that define the quantum world—electrons, photons, quarks, and so forth.

Bob: Of course. How could I have forgotten my quanta?

Cock: You'll be lucky enough to survive the spacetime travel one way. To do it twice means certain death for a physical body as large —and as dense—as yours.

Bob: But what about you—aren't you booked on a round trip package?

Cock: It's different for me. My physical makeup is not as massive as yours. In all likelihood, I'll survive the return trip. Of course, there is a small statistical chance that I won't, but I am willing to take the risk for the good of my species and for the good of the planet.

Bob: I don't like the sound of all this. What if I just say "no" to the whole thing?

Cock: You'll be visited every evening by one of my colleagues. We'll keep coming one by one, night after night, trying to convince you to come back with us until, of course, it all ends for you.

Bob: In other words, I can say "no" tonight, but I'll keep being visited until I say "yes"...or go crazy.

Cock: The latter is definitely a possibility since your reality—these "visitations," as you call them—won't be understood at all by your compatriots.

Bob: It's true...I won't be able to talk about this with anyone...

Cock: In all likelihood, no. And that will be extremely damaging to you. Few humans realize how the inability to clearly articulate what you experience—or the experience of not being believed if you do somehow manage to state it—truly undermines a life.

Bob: I'll be left alone with it all. All this knowledge, all this forewarning...

Cock: ...which will result in self-imposed silence. Hurt. Shame. It's all in your future should you choose to stay.

Bob: I'll go crazy...

Cock: If that is what you mean by "crazy," then, yes, you'll go crazy. Your peers certainly won't understand. Humans seem to have a hard time accepting the unusual, the seemingly inexplicable. It's all part of that "separation-from-nature" problem.

Bob: You're telling me that other creatures, besides humans, would have no problem accepting talking cockroaches from the future?!

Cock: Creatures living in harmony with nature learn to expect the unexpected. You humans would have done well to do the same. As it is, yours is a species that doesn't respond to threats until it's too late.

Bob: I think, given the momentous decision you've put before me, you might—out of courtesy if nothing else—spare me the lectures.

Cock: Of course, my apologies. But really, Bob, the bus is leaving. Now what's it going to be? Yes or no?

Bob: I'm thinking, damn it! I'm thinking!

And then there is silence at the kitchen table while Bob thinks for a good long time.

Part 3 :
A Trip to Minnesota

☢ ⚛ ☢ ⚛ ☢

(Sunset)

Chapter 1:
Bob Agrees to Return to the
Distant Future

The fateful moment arrives. Bob must decide whether to die a horrible death with all his human brothers and sisters or to take a chance at living in an alien civilization where roaches rule the world. Bob considers his options and realizes that he at last understands the concept of "the lesser of two evils."

Bob takes a deep breath—and with his exhale comes an unexpected "yes."

There, a decision made. Bob agrees to go to the distant future. And with only little Cock as his guide.

"Excellent!" exclaims Cock. "Not only have you just saved your own life, but you stand to make enormous contributions to a society that, forgive me for saying so, is many thousands times more advanced than your own."

"Oh well," sighs Bob, "at least I'll get to see how the other half lives. Just see if you can refrain from putting me under a microscope, okay?"

Cock ignores the patter from Bob's lips—knowing that it stems primarily from Bob's nervousness and his inability to understand fully what awaits him—and prepares for the journey the two are about to take together. From behind one set of wings, Cock extracts a tiny circular object and holds it out toward Bob.

"What's that?" Bob asks.

"It's what you must take before our journey. It's a relaxing pill.

It will put your mind to sleep and make your body supple enough to withstand the movement through spacetime."

Bob takes the tiny white tablet from Cock's outstretched leg-arms and examines it. Much to his amazement, on closer inspection, he thinks he can decipher writing on it.

"It says 'aspirin'!" Bob exclaims.

"We thought giving you something that looks familiar would make it easier on you," Cock explains.

"Why, your hospitality knows no bounds, Mr. Cock. But just what, exactly, is this going to do to me?"

Bob is more than a little apprehensive.

"The specifics of it all are much too complicated to go into right now. Either trust me or not, Bob. This is the method to get you back home with me. I just don't have the time or patience anymore to go into every little detail with you."

"All right, don't get touchy," Bob says, "a body just wants to know what goes in it that might end up propelling it into the future."

Here, Cock takes on a slightly schoolmarm-ish tone.

"For clarification's sake, Bob, it's not the pill that takes you to the future. *I* do. But you need to be sedated and your body must be pliable enough for me to escort it through spacetime. Understand?"

"Not at all," Bob says readily. Bob has never minded admitting when he doesn't know something. He has never been one of those guys who are constitutionally unable to ask for directions.

Once again Cock explains as best he can.

"The pill contains a super concentration of some very power-ful substances—opiates, cannabinoids, and phenylethylamine, among others—and it's a significant part of the reason that we can only take you one way. To take the pill and move through spacetime more than once would kill you. You see, given your human anatomy and viscous protoplasm, you're not made for advanced movement through the fabric of spacetime. You humans really are creatures of dense, dense matter and not at all fit for this kind of travel. In fact, if you must know, as we move through spacetime, some of your parts are likely to get 'stuck.'"

Bob is quick to object.

"Stuck?! What do you mean stuck?!"

"Don't worry," Cock assures him, "It's nothing big. Not like an arm or something. It's all on the micro level—a neuron here, an electron there. Maybe a cell or two. Tiny pieces of you will get caught somewhere—it's unavoidable. It's the friction effect. But don't worry, when we arrive at our destination, you will recuperate for several weeks—"

"Several weeks! I thought you said this wasn't dangerous!"

"—and then you'll be fine. A little achy, but fine. And it's not terribly dangerous, it's just mildly dangerous. Not to mention reasonably uncomfortable. But, believe me, it's a whole lot better than what awaits you here."

"What about you?"

"Like I said: It's different for me. I am not a creature of your density."

Bob stops protesting and sits down. He realizes it just doesn't matter any more. He believes his visitor and the apocalyptic predictions about the human species. Bob always anticipated the demise of civilization deep in his bones, anyway. Hearing Cock tell it was more like a confirmation than a revelation. Bob knows if he stays, he dies. So why not take the risk to go forward? Whatever the future holds, even being ripped apart in the blender of spacetime—just change the "frappé" button to "friction"—can't be any worse than dying of radiation or germ poisoning, not to mention being killed by a desperate neighbor trying to steal your last bottle of uncontaminated water.

"Okay," Bob announces after reviewing his options again, "I'm ready."

"Excellent, Bob. You won't regret it. Now take the pill so we may begin."

Obliging, Bob gets up, pours himself a glass of bottled water from the refrigerator, (he hasn't had a drink directly from the tap in years) and washes down his "aspirin" tablet.

"I think you should lie down on the floor," Cock advises.

"Sure, why not," Bob shrugs, "I vacuumed yesterday."

"And take all your clothes off! No use asking for friction trouble!"

Bob strips—remembering to take off his watch, and the college class ring he still wears, in the process—then lies down on the hand-loomed antique kitchen rug his grandmother made and closes his eyes. He breathes deeply, inducing a sort of forced relaxation.

"Good," says Cock, "now, while the effects of the pill are washing over you, I'll build the bug bridge."

"The bug bridge?" Bob asks from the floor. "The journey to the future is taken on a bug bridge?"

"It's just a little joke, Bob."

But the pill is already taking effect. Bob hears himself speaking as if from a distant room.

"Well, I think that it's admirable how you refer to yourselves as 'bugs,'" he manages to say with his rubber tongue. "How charmingly self-deprecating of you."

And here again Cock gently corrects Bob, but it doesn't matter because Bob's body and mind are already in a deep, deep state of suspension:

"Oh, Bob, dear, it's not *we* who are the bugs."

Then Cock finishes his preparations in silence, coaxing the fabric of spacetime to wrap around the duo like a living, breathing cloak, moving them through the fashions of history, from being to nothingness and back again, from the seam of here to the hem of there, and then landing, at last, exactly where Cock left off.

Unexpected Memory Interruption #1:
A Childhood Car Trip

B ob is sitting in the backseat of the family station wagon. His father is driving and scratching himself. His mother is in the front seat next to his father, wearing sunglasses over puffy eyes and looking straight ahead at the lonely two-lane highway that stretches out before them on the deserted midwestern plain. Bob is a child. He is the child of his parents and there is no escaping that oppressive fact—even now, especially now, here on a teary Sunday afternoon drive.

Bob looks out the window at the fields of corn rushing by. His odd little family—as disingenuous and disconnected from each other as it is—is in the midst of performing a family ritual: Driving the back roads to grandma's and grandpa's for Sunday dinner. Dinner, for the uninitiated, takes place in the afternoon, for this is the part of the country where lunch is called dinner and dinner called supper. Bob rebels against these family outings, these rhythms as regular as clockwork —every Sunday, every week, come rain, come snow, come fighting, come tears. If today is Sunday, then we must be in the car on our way to visit grandma and grandpa—this is something Bob knows in his bones.

Bob looks out the window at the fields of corn rushing by. He thinks of his grandma and grandpa. Of late, Bob is shifting his allegiances. For the first part of his young life, he liked his grandmother best. Of course, that was not a difficult decision or one based without self-interest. Bob's grandmother dotes on him. He is the firstborn. And he's a quiet child. And he's bright. And he doesn't show his emotions easily. And Bob's grandmother approves highly of all these things. But as he gets older, Bob thinks he detects something about his grandmother—that she likes the idea of him more than the reality of him. She likes Bob to be around her, but she doesn't seem to take much interest in the particulars of his life. She never wants to hear about his friends or his hobbies. She just wants him there at the family table, saying grace, and telling those funny stories of his.

Bob's grandfather is more stand-offish. He's gruff. He's ornery. He's nobody's fool. And now Bob feels himself more drawn to the gruff distance of his grandfather than the doting favoritism of his grandmother. Bob feels a little guilty about "changing teams." His grandmother has certainly shown him more attention and affection over the years, but right now, at age thirteen, he finds himself just liking his grandfather better.

Bob thinks about these things—and not about the fight his parents just had—as he looks out the window at the fields of corn rushing by. The rows of knee-high corn, moving past, like the spokes of a fan, fanning out, flying by. Like a movie. Like a kaleidoscope. Like a pattern of whizzing perspective—fanning fields—all for the pleasure of his eye.

Bob is an inquisitive child, taking interest in history and the world around him. Bob considers his grandfather to be a specimen from an earlier time, someone who has been to places and worlds Bob cannot even imagine and who can bring to Bob some knowledge of those realms. Bob's grandfather usually isn't so keen on answering Bob's questions about the past—"what's been done let be done," he's often heard his grandfather say—but occasionally Bob will get some nugget from his gruff old grandfather that he treasures and remembers for years at a time.

Once, in just such an inquisitive mood at one of those Sunday family dinners, Bob asked his grandfather what was the greatest invention in his lifetime. By this time, Bob was already enamored with electronics—he had a Super 8 milli-meter camera (with sound), an Atari 8100 computer (that he had put together himself), and a reel-to-reel tape recorder, among other things—and Bob expected for his grandfather to answer something along these lines, things like "the tele-phone," "television," "radio," or even "space travel."

But that's not what Bob's grandfather said.

Even though Bob's grandfather himself was enamored by electronic devices—he was the first of his farmer peers to get a police scanner, and then a citizen's band two-way radio, and later a satellite dish for cable reception—still, Bob's grandfather mentioned none of these things, as amazing as they assuredly were.

Instead, without the slightest hesitation, as if he had been waiting all his life for someone to ask him this very question, Bob's grandfather stated firmly: "aspirin."

Aspirin was the greatest invention in his lifetime.

At first Bob was surprised. Astounded even—or perhaps disappointed. Aspirin was a dime-store staple. One of those things that are embedded in the routines of life—a quintessential object taken for granted.

But, as Bob grew older, as his own aches and pains increased, he found himself thinking of that exchange with his grandfather and understanding—on a deep level, on a visceral level—exactly what the old guy was saying.

And now, in the present, in Bob's current present, with parts of him colliding with the microscopic particles that make up the vast stretches of spacetime, Bob understands as he never has before that his grandfather's answer spoke to the deepest essence of the human condition—to the eternal, essential struggle, the survival of and the tolerance of pain.

Now, as Bob moves unnaturally through the netted mesh of space-coupled-with-time, he understands that experiencing pain is at the heart of being human. It is present at birth, present at death, and regularly present at all times in between. Bob understands, as no human has, that the heart of human struggle is to survive pain—or at least tolerate it long enough to pass along your DNA to another generation who might do a little better in the eternal endeavor.

An endeavor that—seeing how the species finally came to an end—is now over.

But before he can dwell too long on that sad fact—the extinction of the human species—Bob is a child again. Riding in a car. Looking out a window.

Bob looks out the window of his parents' stationwagon as the fields of corn rush by. He calculates how long it will take until his odd, disconnected little family arrives at grandma's and grandpa's for Sunday dinner, his mother explaining away her puffy eyes.

And, while he's at it—since he enjoys numbers, since Bob finds numbers so much more predictable (and therefore so much more comforting) than people—he also calculates his grandfather's current age and his age in the years ahead.

In the year 2000, Bob realizes, his grandfather will be 83 years old. And, God willing, still chomping on his stockpile of aspirin.

Chapter 2:
The Hospitality House

When Bob regains consciousness in the future—waking one morning from unsettling dreams—he's not sure if he's in heaven or hell. He's not even sure he's alive and not dead. But after a few moments, he senses pressure on his backside, from the back of his head all down the length of his body to his heels. He decides he must be alive because he's never heard of a ghost who experienced physical sensations—and terribly painful ones at that.

In fact, Bob is alive. Very much so. As he soon discovers, he is lying down, in a bed on his back, in a totally white room. More importantly, he is aware of every single part of his body—even the microscopic parts that are missing—because every single part of his body hurts. It's not just vague areas such as "leg" or "arm" that hurt. No, the pain is infused throughout specifics such as tissues, tendons, bones, marrow, blood vessels, capillaries—nails and freckles, too.

Bob tries to understand the pain, tries to understand where it comes from. For this is how Bob has always dealt with pain—discover its origins and then use the knowledge as a salve to help ameliorate it. Physical and psychological pain are, for Bob, practically indistinguishable. And right now, the sensation of pain has completely taken over both his body and mind.

But this is not Bob's biggest problem at the moment. The pervasive pain he is feeling is nothing compared to the overwhelming sensation of fear he is about to experience. For, shortly after coming to and beginning to take in his surroundings, including his aches and pains, Bob notices a door in his windowless room, and then he notices that the door begins to open.

Oh, good, thinks Bob, now little Cock will appear and tell me where I am and what is happening.

Sadly, for Bob and his aches and pains, this is not the case.

First of all, the door is roughly the same size door that Bob is used to from human dwellings, a little smaller, perhaps, but not much —certainly something too large for Cock to open. Secondly, a type of cart comes through the door first. Bob can't see the bottom of it, but his mind fills in the image of little wheels or casters rolling it along— but, again, it is something that is too big for Cock to push. And lastly, the actual pusher of the cart appears through the doorway, and it is certainly not Cock.

It is a monstrous vermin.

It is an *ungeheueres Ungeziefer*. A creature who has no place in the family. An unclean animal not suited for sacrifice.

In other words, it is a giant, walking, upright cockroach.

Bob is screaming. Bob is really screaming. Bob is screaming like he has never screamed before. He is too weak to be thrashing and flailing on the bed, but if he had more strength that is exactly what he would be doing.

Instead, he is spastically jerking on the bed, and all the while screaming, screaming, screaming.

Bob's behavior, naturally, is upsetting to the creature. A creature who, by the way, has no conception of itself as monstrous—a creature who, in fact, is likewise having a case of the creeps looking at a moving, vocalizing Bob. A Bob who, up until this point, has been lying there mute and docile for weeks.

Duly startled, the creature accidentally crashes the cart (spilling its contents to the floor) and scurries back and forth in front of Bob's bed. Bob is now forced to experience an up-close viewing of the creature's brown underbelly, sectioned off by arch-shaped ribs, with its many legs waving, willy-nilly, helplessly before Bob's eyes.

Of course, this only serves to elicit larger and louder screams from Bob, thereby increasing the pandemonium all around.

This, finally, is the scene in process when little Cock does appear, arriving on a motorized platform that situates him about eye-level with the bed-stricken Bob.

"What's going on?! What's going on?!" Cock crows as he enters the room and sees Bob wigging out.

Then Cock sees the creature. But as soon as Cock arrives, the creature calms down. Cock instantly surmises what has happened. For a brief moment, the antennae of Cock and the other creature wave furiously at each other and then the thing promptly leaves.

Bob is still heaving in his epileptic terror, but at least his screams have stopped. Cock waits several minutes until Bob's breathing returns somewhat to normal, coming back from the edges of asphyxiation.

"Are you all right?" Cock finally asks.

"What the hell was that?!" sputters Bob.

"That was your nurse," Cock states calmly.

"Nurse?! That was no nurse! That was a monster! Looking for a meal!"

"That was your nurse bringing you a meal. You really must calm down, Bob."

Bob consciously takes a deep breath. It has absolutely no effect on his nerves, so he takes another. And another.

"Don't hyperventilate," warns Cock.

"They're big." Bob states tersely.

"Yes, Bob," Cock answers just as tersely. "We're big."

A dim realization begins to dawn on Bob.

"What are you telling me?" Bob asks, almost not wanting to know.

"We're all big," Cock states firmly. "All except me."

"No!"

It was just as Bob feared.

"I'm sorry," Cock apologizes, "I didn't get a chance to tell you before we left."

"Didn't get a chance?! You bring me to a world of monstrous-sized cockroaches and you didn't get a chance to tell me?!"

"We ran out of time," Cock offers matter-of-factly.

"I think that's something you ought to have mentioned to a fellow! Especially to a fellow who *hates* cockroaches, by the way! Especially *big* ones!"

"Look, it's truly unfortunate the way this has all unfolded. But that's the case. Yes, compared to your domestic cockroaches, our species is bigger than—"

"Bigger?! You're almost human size! With a saddle and a harness, I could ride down to the corner store for some cigarettes! No, make that alcohol. Please, make that some alcohol!"

"Yes, we're bigger than you expected and I'm sorry I didn't get a chance to tell you before we had to leave. But, like I said, we ran out of time. The important thing is that now you know."

"You're big. You're *all* big. A society of big, mother-fucking cockroaches. Is that what I'm hearing? You, you're not the rule—you're the exception?"

"Yes. That's the picture," admits Cock.

"What a hideous picture it is," laments Bob.

Cock is pacing on the platform. Finally Cock says, "Bob, can we move on?"

"I can't even move out of this bed. What other choice do I have?"

"That's the spirit, Bob. Have the courage to accept the things you cannot change."

"Listen," Bob growls, "I don't want them touching me. You got that?"

Bob is quite firm on this point.

"I will be sure to inform everyone of Bob's 'no touch' policy," Cock assures.

For a moment there is silence between them. Bob can't tell if Cock is making fun of him or not, but in the end he decides it doesn't matter. Here he is, stuck in the future, with mammoth-sized cockroaches ruling the Earth. Sarcasm seems to be the least of his problems.

"Where am I?" Bob finally asks.

"You're in the hospitality house," Cock says with pride. "Especially constructed for you."

"Yeah," Bob agrees. "It looks like a hospital. Everything is so white and dreary. I expected an antiseptic smell to go along with it, but there isn't one."

"It's not that there isn't a smell here—antiseptic or not. It's just that you're unable to perceive it. You see, you've lost your sense of smell."

"I've what?!"

"Lost virtually all of your sense of smell. Strong smells held very close to your nose may still register, but nothing else."

"How did that happen?" asks a weary Bob.

"It was part of the friction effect," Cock states. "Most of the quanta pieces that you lost were apparently part of your olfactory system."

"Great."

Bob sniffs the air just to test the veracity of Cock's assertion, and, indeed, he smells nothing.

"It's just as well, Bob," Cock explains. "Our species doesn't smell very good to your species anyway."

"Well, thank heaven for small miracles."

"You're making light of it. But really, it would be quite a problem for you. I know, because, you see, the same is true for us— you don't smell very good to us either. Believe me, it's quite a stench."

Bob is somewhat embarrassed. He has always been afraid of giving off body odors he himself couldn't detect.

"Really?" asks Bob. "What does it smell like?"

Cock thinks a moment.

"Oh, I don't know…it's like a curious mixture of roses and mustard gas."

"Something else to lose sleep over," Bob groans. "Offending the noses of my horrid hosts."

At this notion, little Cock laughs.

"We don't have noses, Bob. Don't you know anything about cockroach anatomy?"

"It's my worst fear that I'm about to find out."

"We 'smell' things through sensors in our scent-receptive antennae. It's all based on chemical impulses."

"How romantic. But if you don't have a nose, then how do you breathe?"

"Through holes in our abdomen which are attached to air tubes. They're called spiracles."

"Oh, the miracles of spiracles," snarls Bob. "Let's strike up the band, shall we?"

"No need to be impolite, Bob. I thought since you'd be living with us the rest of your natural life span—what do you have left? 30, maybe 40 years?—I thought you'd be interested in learning a little more about us. We're full of anatomical marvels—for instance, we have a second brain deep in our bowels that warns us of danger and is connected directly to our legs for flight. Also, we have an amazing gastrointestinal system that allows us to eat virtually anything and derive some kind of nutrition out of it. Would you like to learn more about either of these amazing things?"

Bob lets loose a big sigh and closes his eyes.

"Maybe later, Cock. But not now. As you can see, I'm a little preoccupied with recuperating from time travel and the shock of seeing a disgusting monster!"

Bob is picayune, like a whiny child.

"The proper term is spacetime travel, and the nurse is not a disgusting monster," Cock reprimands.

"Whatever."

There is more uneasy silence between them.

Finally, Bob turns his head to look at Cock, who is still pacing on the contraption that the little roach wheeled in on.

"I'm very concerned about pain management strategies," Bob states gravely.

"What do you mean?" asks Cock, confused.

"Can I get some pain relief? For my unbearable aches and pains?!"

"Of course. Forgive me. What hurts?"

"Everything. Especially the parts that are missing."

"Yes. That would be the phantom effect," Cock explains. "You will have phantom pain in your missing quanta for a little while. But don't worry. We've got the cure for all that ails you."

"I hope it's not some cockroach equivalent of cod liver oil."

"Really, Bob. This is the *hospitality* house, remember? Now, if you think you can stand it, I'll call the nurse in again to bring you some nourishment."

Bob is not sure if he can take seeing the nurse again just yet. His nerves have had one bad jolt after another. So, he stalls for a moment.

"I don't want food. I want pain medication. Can't *you* bring me that?"

Cock waves his antennae side-to-side.

"No, Bob. I'm too small to feed you or administer remedies. If you're not ready to face the nurse yet, then we can wait until you are. But I really think it's in your best interest to have some nourishment as soon as possible."

Bob thinks about the creature hovering over him again. He's not sure he can handle it. But the aches and pains are really getting to him. He doesn't think he can take much more of the discomfort. There is a pounding and a burning racing through every fiber of his being.

Finally, Bob swallows hard and ekes out a whisper.

"Okay," Bob says. "Send her in."

Cock hesitates. There is something Cock needs to explain to Bob. Cock decides it might as well happen now.

"The nurse is not a she," Cock says bluntly.

"Whatever. Like I could tell. I wasn't peeking at any private parts. Just send *him* in."

"The nurse is not a he, either."

Bob did not expect this answer. He raises an eyebrow.

"You have a third gender?"

"That's just it, Bob. We don't have any genders."

Bob's second eyebrow rises to join the first. Now he is really confused.

"What are you talking about?" Bob asks.

"We have reproductive duties, of course, but no genders per se. Each member of society is simply a member of society, with no differentiation. None greater or lesser than the others. We all do our reproductive part as anatomy dictates, of course, but we don't really dwell on the gender aspect of it. Accordingly, we don't use gender pronouns to identify other members of society. We use proper names or, in certain instances, social functions."

At this point, the throbbing in Bob's head matches the throbbing in every other part of his body.

"Whatever the nurse is, just send it in!"

"You're going to have to learn these things before you can go out into society, Bob. We might as well start now."

"Can I just get some relief here, for god's sake?!"

Bob is a man on the verge of a nervous breakdown.

"Of course, Bob. Calm down. I'm just trying to acclimate you to your new surroundings."

"Maybe you should have thought about that *before* we left!"

It is clear that Bob is not pleased with the surprises awaiting him on this end of the journey.

Without addressing this aspect, however, Cock's antennae wave. Almost instantaneously, the nurse appears through the door pushing another cart.

At the site of the nurse, another wave of revulsion washes through Bob—and a gag reflex he can't control overtakes him—but at least he doesn't retch. There's none of the pizza left in his stomach by this point, anyway.

The nurse slowly approaches Bob. Clearly there is curiosity there, and nervousness, too. Up to this point, the nurse—like all other members of Cock's society—has only seen images of creatures like Bob. No living, breathing human to bring to life the mythology associated with them. This is quite a moment—the meeting of two vastly different species over a span of millions of years.

Like a peace offering, the nurse timidly holds out a bowl in front of Bob.

Cautiously, Bob looks down at the bowl, trying to view as little of the creature as possible in the process.

Then, suddenly, Bob's concern over the creature disappears. This is because he is staring into a disquieting bowl of steaming, brown, viscous liquid.

Bob eyes the bowl. Then he looks at Cock. He eyes the bowl again.

He can't help thinking it looks just like a crock of warmed-over feces.

Slowly, Bob says, "What's this?"

"The magic potion that will heal you," Cock answers.

"Okay, but what is it?" Bob insists.

The nurse is still patiently holding the bowl in front of Bob. Cock says, "Try it. You'll like it."

Bob answers with forceful tones, "I'm not touching this. Not until you confirm for me that it's not...not—how shall I say this?—a heaping portion of vile excrement!"

"Excrement?!" Cock ejaculates.

Now Cock is visibly upset, shaking uncontrollably on the motorized platform and pointing an accusatory foreleg at Bob.

"I'd advise you, Bob, to be a little less blasphemous when you get out in the greater society! Now enough of this nonsense! Drink up! Before your strength fades again and we lose you for good!"

Bob is surprised to hear a reference to his impending demise. He dreads—and rightly so it turns out—that his condition is less stable than he had thought. Fearing for his life now, Bob tentatively removes the bowl from the nurse's bristled forelegs—being very careful not to accidentally brush up against any part of the creature—and holds the bowl in front of his face.

"Go ahead," instructs a firm Cock.

After another moment of hesitation, Bob slowly brings the bowl to his lips.

He closes his eyes and bravely takes a sip.

Suddenly, Bob's eyes pop back open as the feeling of something old and familiar slides past his happy tongue and down his equally happy throat.

"Hey," he announces with shock. "It tastes just like hot cocoa!"

Calm again, Cock nods his antennae.

"Yes, Bob. Civilizations may come and go, but the love of chocolate endures."

Bob slurps down several more gulps before speaking again.

"My god, where did you get chocolate from?"

Bob finishes the bowl as Cock answers his question.

"We found young cacao seedlings frozen in a glacier in the Ulua Valley—a once-luscious province in what used to be northwestern Honduras. It was once a great cacao bean producing region—during your human era, that is. We were able to extract one of the seedlings from its fortuitous time capsule and graft its genetic structure onto a host plant that could survive in our era. Now we have fields of the stuff. It's our main staple. Our sacred food."

"Hardly excrement," Bob notes cheerily.

"Hardly," Cock intones. "We've modified the formula a bit, so that now it's full of protein, glycogen, and other nutrients we need, not to mention all kinds of medicinal properties that will stop all your pain and facilitate your healing within seconds. Also, specially for you, we've added a high percentage of glucose. However, we like to drink it bitter, adding chilies and spices to make an enticing, frothy beverage, similar to how the original Mayans preferred it."

Bob is smacking his lips and listening attentively.

"It was a more concentrated version of this that we gave you in the spacetime pill to get you here."

"Really?"

Cock continues, "Yes. The high doses of phenylethylamine are especially helpful regarding healing and spacetime travel—it's a chemical that mimics the brain chemistry of being in love, a state of extreme suggestibility and almost endless potential."

"What?" asks Bob.

"When you're in love, you can do anything—including moving the boundaries of spacetime. Yes, it's kind of like applying a shoehorn to spacetime travel, a shoehorn of love."

"Amazing," Bob concludes as he hands the empty bowl back to the nurse creature who has been waiting patiently for Bob to finish. Now with his belly full of the perfect food, the nurse seems slightly—but only slightly—less disgusting to Bob. Indeed, Bob will need a lot more cocoa before he develops charitable, let alone *loving*, feelings toward the nurse.

Regardless, the nurse puts the bowl back on the cart, waves its antennae at Cock, and then pushes the cart out the door.

With equal parts horror and fascination, Bob watches the creature leave, staring at its amazing brown convex backside, with its two pairs of great leathery, transparent wings swaying gently with its upright motion.

Breaking Bob's mesmerized spell, Cock reports, "The nurse is pleased you like the potion so much. It was a special recipe, handed down for millions of generations, and then modified especially for your metabolism."

Bob is confused. He didn't hear anything.

"How do you know all that?"

"No, you didn't hear anything. And you won't. Except maybe a song now and then, but I'll explain that to you later."

"What are you talking about?" Bob asks.

"Exactly," Cock says. "I'm talking about talking. Our species doesn't talk, so to speak."

"How do you communicate?" asks Bob, stupefied.

"Through electromagnetic impulses relayed through our antennae."

"Telepathy?"

"Yes. I believe that's your word for it. We just call it think-casting."

Bob is confused.

"But you can talk to me. Why don't you talk to each other?"

Now little Cock is really shaking with laughter.

"That's a good one, Bob! Talk to each other! Instead of think-casting! How you do amuse me when you're not exasperating me!"

"I don't see what's so funny."

"No, probably not. Clearly you know nothing about the joys of think-casting. Otherwise, you'd never suggest we engage in something so primitive as talking."

"Primitive? It's hardly primitive. It's what separated humans from all other creatures."

"No, you just think it did, Bob."

Ignoring the comment, Bob continues, "But you can talk to me. Can't others?"

"No. I had to undergo extensive anatomical reconstruction in order to be able to communicate with you in a way that you'd understand. No one else would do it if they didn't have to, and now that I've returned from your time intact, no one else has to. So now, not only am I the Bringer of Bob, but I'm your translator, too."

"'Bringer of Bob?'"

"That's my official designation now. An honorific, if you will. The sign of a mission well accomplished."

"Well, Mr. Cockroach Hudson, Bringer of Bob—does that make you the only person, er, being, I can communicate with?"

"Not exactly, Bob. You see, most of your thoughts will be accessible to most of us like an open book. I only translate *from* our species *to* you. Everyone in our society will be able to, basically, read your every thought before you even speak it. Of course, that's not to mention the thoughts you may have that you weren't planning on speaking."

"What?! Am I to have *no* privacy?!" Bob wails.

"Luckily for you, because your brain waves are so rudimentary —they diffuse quickly once outside the protective cocoon of your skull—our species will have to be in close physical proximity to you in order to tune-in to your thoughts. So, as long as you're alone— within a radius of five feet, say—you should have all the privacy you need. By the way, the dimensions of this room are ten by ten and your bed is in the center. So, as long as you're recuperating, and no one else is in the room with you, you'll have your thoughts all to yourself."

Bob crashes back into his pillow.

I can't believe this, he thinks.

"I know you can't," Cock answers. "But you'll get used to it. Now get some rest and I'll see what I can do about getting you a spot on tomorrow's program. Everyone is eager to meet you."

Unexpected Memory Interruption #2:
Welcome to *Bleakerville!*

B ob is sleeping—and dreaming. And just like a dream, it all makes perfect, illogical logical sense.

It's a big, flashy fantasy of a dream, featuring a busy soundstage full of assistants wearing headphones rushing to and fro with clipboards in front of them and looking very, very important. There are lights, there are cameras, and suddenly there is the stillness before real action.

Bob is taking it all in, standing off to the side in a type of makeshift green room. And—for reasons he doesn't understand—he finds himself sitting in a type of mechanized cart that has been adorned in all sorts of decorative ways, including a hood ornament that sports a profile of the god Apollo. Having seen "Ben Hur" several times, Bob can only think to describe the contraption as a motorized Roman chariot sporting the tail-fin panache of a '57 Chevy.

While Bob continues to absorb the milieu, the atmosphere changes. Something big is about to happen. Bob can feel it. Suddenly there is a hush. The assistants scurry away out of sight. The lights go down. A big kettle-drum drumroll ripples through the air.

Without warning, there is a magnificent burst of light, followed by sound and fury, and then a man appears from nowhere ensconced in a tight spotlight. He wears a fez and a white shirt, white leggings, and a white skirt. Most noticeable of all, he is twirling—amazingly fast. He is barefoot—holding his arms out in ecstatic, passionate gestures—with his white skirt billowing as he twirls.

Suddenly, he stops. With practiced precision, he looks dead-on into the camera following him.

"Hello, honored guests! And welcome to *Bleakerville!*"

An audiotape of an audience clamoring wildly is pumped into the empty studio.

"I'm your host, the whirling dervish of Koyna, Jalaluddin Rumi, and I'm happy to welcome you to the game show where contestants from all over the galaxy quiz each other on the nature of their local realities!"

The dervish Rumi is a very handsome fellow, Bob notes, with his trim beard and swarthy complexion. He cuts quite an impressive figure with his athletic body neatly tucked into his red fez and white outfit. And, even better, Rumi emanates a greater sense of peace and well-being than most other game show hosts Bob has observed.

"Let's meet our first guest," Rumi announces, "the challenger who hails from a little blue-green and white dot in the unfashionable end of the galaxy's western spiral. Won't you please give a warm welcome to—appearing all the way from Minnesota USA—Bob Bridges!"

An audio track of an audience clapping riotously fills the soundstage as Bob's little motorized chariot rolls itself, and Bob, into the spotlight next to Rumi.

"We're so glad you could be here this evening, Mr. Bridges."

"Oh, please call me Bob."

"Surely, Bob."

Bob is about to make an old joke, but he's not sure how well it will translate on cosmic airwaves, so he thinks better of it and holds his tongue.

Instead, he answers, "I'm not really sure where I am, but I'm darn glad to be here."

"Spoken like a true intrepid West-Ender!" shouts Rumi. "Let's have a big *Bleakerville* welcome for Bob

Bridges!"

Rumi himself claps, as the clapping audio track joins him, and Bob's little motorized chariot wheels itself over to a slightly elevated dais inscribed, simply: "Bob from Minnesota."

Bob settles into his spot while Rumi makes a faux aside to the nonexistent audience. "Now isn't he a charmed and charming little fellow?" Then Rumi's voice gets louder, building into another shout. "But, still, he's probably no match for our returning champion!"

Fake laughter fills the stage, as Bob gets a determined look on his face. We'll see about that, Bob thinks.

Rumi winks at Bob and then continues.

"And now, without further ado, I give you our undefeated champ, who hails from deep within the churning fireball of stars that make up the center of our very own Milky Way galaxy—won't you please give it up for the great Swami of Swamis, our very own Sheep Herder Numero Uno!"

The audiotape goes wild with the sound of throngs cheering, screaming, and clapping. It's a moment to rival the Beatles at Shea Stadium, Bob thinks. And to complete the effect, spotlights criss-cross the stage frenetically while the drumroll reaches an unbearable crescendo.

But nothing happens.

The moment of anticipation is over and the noise dies down to the sounds of silence.

Then, without warning, a beautiful man, also with a trim beard and swarthy features, descends from the studio skywalk in a cloud of bluish-white gas. When his bare feet at last touch the floor of the stage, the elegant man, who is wrapped in crisp white bolts of cloth, reverently bows his head.

This slick, showman's entrance is greeted with

thundering, but still artificial, applause. Bob can be seen in the background crossing his arms and rolling his eyes.

Like they can't see the wires, Bob thinks wryly.

Rumi rushes over to the man's side and pumps his hand.

"Welcome to you, Swami!"

"Thank you, Rumi. Always a pleasure to be here."

They chat amiably for a few seconds. It seems to Bob that these two gents know each other from way back. Bob is just on the verge of feeling left out, when suddenly the Swami of Swamis, Sheep Herder Numero Uno, takes his place at his own slightly elevated dais, inscribed simply: "Swami."

Without missing a beat, Rumi steps back and throws one arm up, indicating a large screen on the stage. Instantly, a huge image of the Earth appears, surrounded by the lonesome blackness of space.

"Bob Bridges, for ten karmic points, can you tell us the correct name of this ancient being?"

Bob is a little confused by the question. But the image is so clearly of his home planet—it's that astonishing photo Bob is familiar with of the Earth rising over the Moon, the one taken by the Apollo 8 astronauts during their orbit of the Moon on Christmas Eve 1968—that he can think of only one thing to say.

"The Earth," Bob offers positively.

The dervish begins ecstatically whirling again, and shouts out, "No! I'm sorry, Bob! That is incorrect!"

The dervish stops as quickly as he began and looks at the returning champion.

"Swami, would you like to take a crack at this one?"

"Certainly, Rumi." Without even having to think, the Swami answers, "I believe the correct etymology of that being is: Elizabeth Terra Gaia."

"Correct-a-mundo!" roars the host. "And that puts you in the lead by one million and ten karmic points!"

The taped multitude roars its approval.

"Hey, wait a minute!" shouts Bob over the din. He turns to Rumi. "I thought you said the question was worth only ten points?"

"Yes, Bob," the Rumi explains patiently, "but your contestant came in with a bit of a surplus!"

The fake audience laughs appreciably.

Then Rumi turns to the camera and beams, pointing to the Swami of Swamis, Sheep Herder Numero Uno.

"Because the Swami has scored over a million points, he's now in the position to ask our challenger a double-whammy inquiry!"

There are compelling "ooh's" and "aah's" from the nonexistent audience, as the dervish begins to expertly whirl again and then stop. The instant his feet stop, his mouth begins shouting.

"And as you know, my friends, no returning champ has ever had enough points to pose a double-whammy inquiry to a first-time challenger in several millennia! Congratulations, Swami!"

The Swami of Swamis, Sheep Herder Numero Uno, takes a small bow.

Bob immediately breaks out into a sweat.

The Swami turns to Bob and eyes him craftily.

Bob's sweating increases tenfold.

"Don't worry, Bob," the host Rumi reassures, "this is for instructive purposes only!"

Bob wishes that the Rumi would stop shouting.

The dervish then turns to the champ and shouts even louder, "Let 'er roll, Swami!"

Then the Swami of Swamis, Sheep Herder Numero

Uno, clears his swan-like throat and asks Bob directly, "What is the primary dominant activity on your home planet, Elizabeth Terra Gaia?"

Bob's river of perspiration launches into a cascade. He intuitively understands that answering this question incorrectly will result in grave and dire consequences.

Bob thinks hard.

The audio track brings up a loud ticking of a clock.

Bob thinks harder. And harder.

The host interrupts Bob's stalled thinking process.

"Bob, I'm afraid your time is almost—"

"Business!" Bob screams for all he's worth. "Business! Making money! Work! That's our primary activity!"

Bob looks expectantly at the Swami and at Rumi. There is a moment of suspenseful silence. Then Rumi breaks it.

"No! I'm sorry, Bob! That is incorrect!"

But Rumi doesn't appear to be sorry at all. In fact, Rumi looks ecstatic. But, then, the dervish is whirling again, and, Bob reasons, a whirling dervish is supposed to be ecstatic. After all, that's his job.

Suddenly, Rumi stops his twirling and gets very serious.

"The correct answer to the question," Rumi intones, "is sleeping. The primary dominant activity of your home planet, Bob, is sleeping."

"What?!" cries Bob.

The host looks down at the index cards he carries in his hand to make sure there has not been a mistake.

"It says right here that you each spend a third of your life sleeping. That's more than any other single activity. You may make a formal inquiry challenge, but this condition seems to be well-known."

"But I just read in *The New York Times* that Americans are sleeping less and working more!" Bob insists.

"Sorry, Bob," Rumi corrects, consulting his index cards again. "It seems that 'work' is a generic term that encompasses many constituent parts—commuting, talking on the telephone, faxing, photocopying, having lunch, going to meetings, going to the bathroom, and actual labor. Work, therefore, is a manufactured conglomerate of many separate activities, whereas sleeping is one holistic activity. Again, Bob, the correct answer to the question is: sleeping!"

Bob knows he is sunk. He just doesn't know how far yet. So, he lets it go.

Seeing no further challenge from Bob, Rumi turns to the Swami of Swamis, Sheep Herder Numero Uno.

"Congratulations, Swami! You remain our exalted, undefeated champ! And now, you may assume your Grand Prize—the right to pontificate at will!"

The taped audience bursts into recorded cheers.

Then the Swami of Swamis, Sheep Herder Numero Uno, wraps his steely gaze on the sweating and trembling Bob. Bob has never been directly pontificated at by a superior being before, and he's certain it's not going to be at all pleasant.

Bob's worst fears are confirmed as the Swami launches into the following recitation of supreme philosophical truths:

> For millions of years, Bob, intelligent beings have been searching for kindred spirits in a vast and lonely universe. Only on occasion, however, do we succeed. For, while the universe does have intelligent life spread throughout it, the statistical occurrence is not as prevalent as one might think. Therefore,

when candidates of intelligence are discovered, there is great rejoicing among the heavens. Such a time of joy occurred recently when my people discovered your species. However, upon closer observation, a great debate arose about whether you actually exhibited the bare minimum standards to qualify as a bona fide member of the great web of intelligent life. In trying to ascertain this delicate distinction, we eventually asked ourselves, 'With what activity do these creatures primarily occupy themselves?' We knew that the answer to this question would settle the debate. And it did. A subsequent investigation confirmed that your predominant form of activity was sleeping. We realized this primary state of being was merely a metaphor, indicative of your lack of consciousness about yourselves and the world around you. The debate was therefore irrevocably settled: you do not qualify as genuine intelligent life. And, I might add, Bob, that your sad performance here on today's show has only served to confirm that fact.

At this point, Bob knows full well that he does not like being pontificated at. But, instead of running for the high hills—or, better yet, simply waking up—he makes a huge tactical mistake and tries to defend his species.

"All right Mr. High and Mighty Swami. If sleeping is so distasteful as a meaningful occupation, just what, then, do you folks do all day?"

"Beg your pardon?" the Swami asks incredulously. The interruption, let alone the insurrection, has completely caught him off guard.

"I said, Mr. Swami," Bob repeats accusingly, "just what, pray tell, is your primary form of activity?"

The Swami answers proudly and without hesitation.

"Why, swimming, of course."

"Swimming?!" Bob cries.

"Yes, Bob. Swimming."

The Swami is absolutely sure of this point.

"You spend your days and nights swimming? What are you, a bunch of exercise freaks?!"

At this point, the dervish begins whirling feverishly and chanting, "Om, Shanti, Om" at the top of his lungs. He's so excited that he simply cannot contain himself. He hasn't had a show this thrilling in centuries. He's sure to be able to leverage the ratings coup into a big karma hike, he thinks gleefully. Maybe he can get out of the game show business entirely. Maybe he can translate his good fortune into hosting one of those prestigious fix-up-your-planet shows. The possibilities at this point are virtually endless. He spins faster and faster, at last achieving his lifelong quest of religious rapture.

Ignoring Rumi, the Swami continues.

"It's not for exercise, Bob, or even necessarily for something so elemental as pleasure. Instead, it's a form of generating the lifeforce itself."

"Call me all wet, but I just don't get it," says Bob, throwing his hands up.

"I should think not. But perhaps one day you will. You see," the Swami explains, "when someone is spiritually evolved enough on our planet—and at this point, nearly all of us are—they spend their days and nights swimming. It creates life energy. It's a high form of meditative, repetitive motion all in service of a greater goal. And that's good for everyone. And, of course, if someone is especially evolved, then a sheep is placed around their neck as they swim—

"A sheep!" Bob interrupts. "Oh, come on! You're really just pulling my leg here, aren't you? Somebody's going to come out from behind that curtain any minute and hit me over the head with a frozen leg of lamb and end all this nonsense, aren't they?"

"I have no idea what you're talking about," the Swami warns. "But if you keep quiet and listen for a moment, you might learn something."

Bob feels a little sheepish himself, having been admonished by the Swami, so he tries one more time to remain quiet.

"The sheep spins out a great golden coat as the swimmer completes laps," the Swami explains. "The coat is then worn by the swimmer, when not in the process of swimming, as a golden badge of courage and honor. It's a great, great accolade and a holy activity. Why, we have millions of beings engaged in it right now."

Bob simply cannot contain himself.

"Begging your holy pardon and all," he snaps, "I'll just wait for the video to come out."

A dark cloud passes over the furrowed brow of the Swami.

Tiring of Bob's antics, an exasperated Swami turns and speaks authoritatively to Rumi, "It's time for this charade to end."

Rumi immediately stops whirling.

"As you wish, Mighty Swami," he says with a bow. It doesn't matter to Rumi anymore how this turns out. He's already had the success he needs to move on to greener pastures.

The Swami wraps his fearsome gaze on Bob, who

immediately comes to an instinctive, reverential silence. In a mighty voice, the Swami booms, "And now I shall tell you the three sure truths about this universe. Even though you are a creature of much fear and great ignorance, I know that in your heart you wish to know the truth. And so now, here they are, the three sure things we know:

1) There is intelligence woven throughout the universe on every level, macro and micro; as a consequence, there are local manifestations of concentrated pockets of intelligence which show up as certain species;

2) also as a consequence of this, planets themselves are organisms and the locus of intelligence, as are, of course, stars and galaxies; and finally,

3) your Earth — as long as it is infested and maligned by you unconscious creatures of extensive sleep — will remain a dismal, drab, and conflicted place."

With this last mighty utterance, everything around Bob disappears. The Swami—gone. Rumi—gone. The stage and the very chariot beneath Bob—gone. *Bleakerville*, in its entirety—gone.

In its place, Bob finds himself floating naked and helpless—like a babe trapped in an indifferent womb. In the dark belly that is the cold vacuum of space, he shivers and turns to comfort himself, but succeeds only in creating an infinite tumbling, a rolling that extends over and over, without friction and, thus, without end. As he turns, from the corner of his eye, Bob can see the Earth, a luscious blue dot in infinite blackness, an oasis in the void, a single poem on the stark blackboard of time.

Chapter 3:
A Walk Around Town

The next morning, Bob awakes—stumbling out of another round of his species' primary, dominant activity—and discovers that he has an enormous, splitting headache. He also finds that his sheets are soaked and his pillows are on the floor. The evening has been a rough one for Bob.

Bob is bemoaning this unhappy state of affairs to himself when Cock arrives on his motorized platform. Much to Bob's dismay, Cock is particularly gay this morning.

"Hello, my friend," Cock greets Bob jauntily. "How did you sleep?"

"I've slept better," Bob says gruffly. He is still in the process of sorting out his inner turmoil.

"Sorry to hear it," Cock responds cheerfully. "It's a good thing it's time for your morning rations, then. Shall I summon the nurse?"

"Can I have a moment to compose myself?" Bob asks, trying to shake off the early morning dream.

"Certainly," Cock says. "There's a water closet behind that small door. You should find everything you need, I trust."

"Thank you." A naked and exhausted Bob slides out of bed and trots to the bathroom. "I'll be back in a few moments," he calls over his shoulder.

"Take your time," Cock answers. "I'll be waiting!"

It's all just a little too perky for Bob's tastes.

When Bob returns a few minutes later, there Cock stands, as promised—still cheery, still pert.

"Ready?" Cock asks, as Bob climbs back into the bed.

Bob's mood is little improved.

"Ready," Bob replies anyway, smoothing out the covers.

At that, the nurse strolls into the room, carrying a piping hot bowl for Bob. Bob extracts the bowl—again, being careful not to touch or view the creature—and finishes it quickly. He is amazed at how delicious the liquid is and how good it instantly makes him feel.

If only we could bottle this, Bob thinks, smiling to himself.

"We have," replies Cock.

This stirs Bob from his chocolate-induced euphoria and he yells indignantly, "Stop doing that!"

"Doing what?" Cock asks, surprised.

"Answering my thoughts. I was thinking to myself. Not to you."

"Oh, sorry," says Cock. "Unfortunately, with you I can't tell. We have a way of coding our thoughts so that private ones are labeled private and public ones public. But with you, they're all readable. I keep forgetting. Remind me again if I slip."

"No doubt," says Bob, handing the bowl back to the nurse.

Now that the chocolate has made him feel better, Bob decides to risk a short gaze at the creature and looks up. Staring back at him is a disgusting, nearly human-sized roach head that is wholly concealed by a shield-like pronotum, a convex plate of chitin that, in the nurse's case, is tattooed with a distinctive marking of a plant, presumably a cocoa plant. Even more disturbing, and reaching out from under the back of the head, are the bristly labial palps, looking much like the hairy fingers they serve as, to push food into the roach's mouth.

Bob screams.

He realizes that his furtive gaze has been met by a set of anatomical features that could be the very poster child for *UGLY*. In short, he is sorry he looked.

But it is too late—the nurse rushes from the room, dropping the empty rations bowl.

"The nurse is a sensitive creature," Cock chides. "If you can't think something nice, Bob, then don't think anything at all."

Bob forgot that the nurse could read his thoughts, too.

"Uh, sorry," Bob offers lamely.

"I'll let the nurse know that you apologized."

"Thanks."

"So," Cock starts again, this time a little less perky, "are you feeling better?"

"Yes. Much. Thank you."

"Ready for your big day?"

"I suppose," Bob answers guardedly. But in truth, he's feeling almost chipper from the medicinal effects of the ration, and he's eager to see the brave new world before him. "What's on the agenda?" a curious Bob wants to know.

"Let's see," Cock teases. "Nothing out of the ordinary for Bob: just a stroll through a new civilization, seeing some of the sites of the new Earth, and then being the guest of honor at the morning program."

"Oh my," Bob says, also teasing. "What shall I wear?"

At this, Cock laughs heartily. "Oh, Bob. You are a funny one!"

Now the nurse enters Bob's room again, this time carrying a type of space suit. The nurse drops the one-piece outfit, complete with transparent head sack, at the end of Bob's bed, and then promptly leaves the room.

Bob swears he can detect an air of perturbation.

I'm sorry you're so ugly, he thinks as loud as he can.

"It's too late, Bob," says Cock. "Your weak brainwaves are out of antennae shot. Besides, that hardly qualifies as a real apology."

"Well, it's the best I can manage under the circumstances," Bob notes. Then he points to the object at the foot of his bed. "What's that?"

"It's your protection suit from radiation," explains Cock. "You must wear it at all times when you're not in the hospitality house."

"Why?" asks Bob amazed.

"Otherwise, you would vaporize instantaneously. For humans, it's a fryer out there."

Bob is alarmed to hear that the Earth is no longer hospitable for humans. He knows he should have expected it, given what Cock has already told him. But to actually be here, in the future, and not be able to walk on the Earth without protection is a reality that is almost too painful to process. It takes Bob a long moment to gather his thoughts. Cock lets him do so in silence.

Finally, his mind more clear, Bob sets himself to the task at hand, pouring himself into the suit—which he discovers is lightweight and feels like cashmere against his skin—and zips, buckles, and tucks himself in place.

"Let's go," Bob says as he heads for the door.

"Wait a minute." Cock stops him.

Bob turns.

"See that pocket above your heart?"

Bob looks down and sees a stiffened pocket protruding in the area of his upper left chest. It looks vaguely like a balcony.

"Yes. What is it?"

"It's my perch. Kindly put me in it."

Bob is now very happy to be covered head to toe, not one speck of flesh exposed, so that he has absolutely no possibility of actually touching Cock or any other of the mammoth cockroaches he's about to meet. In a perverse way, he's suddenly thankful for the radiation situation that requires an absolute barrier between him and his hosts.

Bob moves to the motorized platform and stretches out his hand, allowing Cock to march onto his palm. Then Bob sweeps his hand up to his chest and little Cock crawls into the chamber—looking vaguely like a dachshund teetering on a car door to get its schnoz out the window, Bob muses.

"Very funny," says Cock about Bob's unspoken image. "Let's just start our day without the critter commentary, shall we?"

Bob smiles—this mind-reading thing has its pluses as well as its minuses—and the duo heads out the door.

Bob and Cock are in an elevator, heading up. Trouble is, they've been doing so for quite some time.

"Where have I been?" asks Bob, amazed at the length of the ride.

"Deep under ground in a chamber made of lead blocks," Cock informs him. "It was just a precaution to protect you from the radiation while you were recuperating. But now that you're tolerating the cocoa rations, the Earth suit should protect you just fine. Relax, we'll be there soon."

"There" happens to be the surface of the Earth—and right on cue, as soon as Cock stops speaking, the elevator stops and the doors slide open.

However, stretched out before him is a scene that Bob can hardly fathom, let alone enter.

"What are you waiting for Bob? Let's go."

Cock can't imagine why they are just standing there.

But Bob has seen the future. And it's not something his brain knows what to do with.

After additional prodding from Cock, Bob takes a small step out of the elevator. Then he stops and slowly turns his head in an 180 degree arc, peering in horrified amazement at the great gray jungle all around him.

It is as if Bob has stepped out into an other-worldly Amazon, and instead of everything being lush and green, all vegetation is gray and washed out, sickly and anemic.

There are dilapidated ferns as big as trees and single frail stalks of plants as tall as lightposts. It is thick and dense—but deathly and eerie—all at the same time. And, just as unnerving, thousands of cockroach inhabitants dart in and out the ghostly plant growth, scurrying here and there, presumably going about their daily duties.

But more than the uncanny feeling that he is inside an oversized nightmare of a terrarium, it is the color of the world itself than frightens Bob—everything is subsumed in ashen shades, including the sky, or at least what little of it Bob can see through the towering and overlapping vegetation. Bob cannot even tell if it is day or night —everything is gray and wan, a ghostly world colored in shades of black and white, and over it all, on the plants, on the ground, lightly falling from the sky, are fine particles of gray dust and ash gently settling on all that exists.

Ironically, it is the cockroaches, with their dark brown and black body tones, who bring the most color to the place. And that, Bob finds, is the most horrifying thing of all. For, given the ungodly grayish state of the world, these creatures are the most interesting, if not the most beautiful, things in it.

Bob shudders at the thought.

Cock doesn't say anything to Bob. Instead, the little guide lets Bob absorb it all as best he can.

As Bob continues to stare dumbfounded at the alien landscape, a huge floating sphere drifts by in the breeze. Bob thinks it looks vaguely like a microscopic spore, or a dandelion tuft, that has been enlarged to the size of a beach ball.

And now the irrepressible scientist that is inside the heart of Cock can remain silent no longer. "That's exactly what it is, Bob. A radiation spore."

"A radiation spore," repeats a fascinated Bob. "Does it give off radiation?"

"Heavens, no! Just the opposite. It bounces along the winds and soaks up radiation, the way a sponge soaks up water. We gather them when they get trapped in atmospheric eddies, and then use them in our sacred ceremonies."

This is all just a little more information than Bob is prepared to handle, so he concentrates instead on the old familiar activity of putting one foot in front of the other.

"Where are we going?" asks Bob, changing the topic as he gingerly steps down the path that has been especially constructed for him to navigate this hideous pseudo-tropical world.

"Currently, in the wrong direction," Cock notes. "Could you go the other way?"

As requested, Bob turns—only to be stopped by what gathers before him.

The denizens of this gray jungle community have not failed to notice Bob on his walkabout, and, fascinated by their guest, they are gathering in droves.

Immediately, Bob experiences a painful shortness of breath. His heart palpitates.

They are moving toward him like a big, dark ocean.

"For the love of God, Cock—tell them to back off!" Bob screeches in raspy tones.

Cock had not expected Bob to be so agitated. This is because Cock has severely underestimated the human capacity to be grossed out by pigmy-sized cockroaches—especially large hordes of pigmy-sized cockroaches that crowd around vying for a good look at the terrified human in question.

But, hearing the clear distress in Bob's voice, Cock does that little trick with the antennae and the crowd slowly begins to back off. The black-bodied mass steps aside, almost as one organism, parting along the path so Bob can drudge onward, with his newfound fans now equidistant in organized rows on either side of him.

"How's that?" Cock asks. "Can you make it through that, Bob?"

Bob is still breathing heavy. In fact, Cock is a little seasick from all the heaving of Bob's chest.

"I don't think so," he gasps. "Can't they all just climb back under the rocks they climbed out from?!"

"Mostly they climbed out from under various decaying fronds, if you want to be accurate," Cock says dryly.

"I don't want to be accurate!" Bob cries. "I want to be alone! Get these monsters out of here!"

"Really, Bob," Cock says with exasperation. "You need more chocolate. You're acting disgraceful in front of a harmless, curious constituency who wants nothing more than to honor you for coming to our world and helping to solve an age-old mystery. The least you could do is refrain from insulting our feelings, if you can't respond graciously to our quite natural curiosity and interest."

Bob is trying. Bob is really trying. He's even trying to think of these creatures in people-like terms. But he just can't bring himself there yet. They are so disgustingly horrifying to him, that he simply can't get over his instinctual dread. He is finally getting used to Cock —yes, that is true. But Cock has the distinct advantage, in Bob's eyes, of being an appropriate minuscule size.

"Yes, yes," Bob finally says, groping for diplomacy. "Please tell them that I am…greatly honored by their interest. But right now I just need a little downtime—"

"Down time? What's down time?" Cock interrupts.

"Decompression time," explains Bob through his panting. "I just need a little more time to adjust before I can meet the masses face to, er, roach head. Okay?"

Bob is pleading and Cock hates to see humans plead. It's so undignified. Any second, Cock half expects to see Bob take off running with his hands waving helplessly in the air.

"All right, all right," Cock says. "I'll ask them to disperse. But some might linger on, especially the younger ones, and in the meantime you've got to come to grips with your new neighbors. Face it, Bob—we're all you've got left."

Bob is wishing that Cock hadn't put it that way. It's the razor-edged truth that he's been trying to avoid ever since he faced the nurse and landed in this grotesque universe.

These are my new people, my new tribe, Bob tries to tell himself as the sweat pours down his forehead. I really ought to stop insulting them before they decide to eat me. In fact, I really ought to be thankful they haven't eaten me already!

"We're vegetarians, Bob!" Cock cries, trying to shake Bob from the bad place he has stumbled into.

But it doesn't help. Bob has clearly fallen deeply into the bad place, and he most certainly can't get up.

At this point, Cock crawls out of his perch and up onto Bob's head bubble. Cock feels the necessity of looking Bob in the eye to bring him back to reality.

"Look, Bob," Cock says soothingly. "Maybe this isn't such a good idea, yet."

"Roger, Einstein!" Bob screams. The few paces that he's taken in this new world have been a bit much for Bob's fragile human heart and overwhelmed human brain—not to mention his pumped-out adrenal system.

"Let's go back to the hospitality house, shall we?" coos Cock. "We'll have a nice hot cup of chocolate and reconvene tomorrow, okay?"

Cock is speaking as if to a frightened child.

"Get back in your perch!" Bob screams. "You're creeping me out!"

Cock scurries away, sensing that Bob is on the edge.

"Okay, Bob, back to the elevator!" Cock commands, realizing there is no time to waste. "We've got to get you some cocoa—and fast!"

Luckily, Bob and Cock are only a few steps from the elevator, which is waiting patiently for them with open doors. Bob rushes inside and collapses into a nerve-shattered mess in the corner.

Quietly, the elevator doors close on a world that is clearly going to take some getting used to for its newest, visiting life-form.

Unexpected Memory Interruption #3: Fast Food, Anyone?

Bob is driving and driving. He's on one of those lonely cross-country trips between his college and his mother's house—after his parents' divorce—during spring or winter break. The total trip is about eighteen hours, door to door, with the only things to keep him company being cassette tapes he's listened to a hundred times before and the long, flat stretches of road before and behind him.

It's a little game Bob plays with himself—to see how quickly he can make the trip. Oh, not in terms of speeding —though, of course, he does that, too. But in terms of stopping. How few stops can he make between here and there? How few stops can he make while he is neither here nor there?

In fact, Bob doesn't make many stops. His stamina is quite good—but, then, why shouldn't it be? After all, he's 18 years old, athletic and in good health, and extremely comfortable behind the wheel. If only his bladder were larger or his thirst not so great. Then he could really set some records.

Anyway, this time—somewhere in the Vowel Belt, somewhere between Akron, Ohio and Terre Haute, Indiana —Bob gives in to his basic urges and pulls off the interstate at the next food-gas-lodging exit.

This being what it is and all, there is nothing much off the exit except a few gas stations, a few fast food restaurants, and a no-frills motel. It could be almost any exit in almost any part of the country. Bob knows this and is somewhat depressed by it, for reasons he can't quite yet articulate — but he will be able to, mind you, when he's in graduate school and reads a book (*City of Quartz*) by a well-known social critic on the architecture of public space.

But enough of this—right now Bob has needs.

Even though Bob hates their food, he always goes to the same ubiquitous fast food chain whenever he stops at an exit. He does this for one reason and one reason only: the blueprint of each franchise is exactly the same and so Bob always knows exactly where the men's restroom is—and, besides, it's generally cleaner than the ones in gas stations. (Okay, so that's two reasons.) Hell, lots of times Bob doesn't even order anything—not even a soda—he just goes in, whizzes, and is back in the car before you can say "cheeseburger in paradise." That's how much he hates their food. Sometimes, even, he'll pee at this restaurant and order a soft drink at the drive-up window of the other one. That's how much he hates their greasy, god-damned, stick-a-toy-in-it, plastic-wrapped, gristle-filled, cartilage-packed, incredible inedible food.

Anyway, this time is not such a time, since Bob is on the last leg of his trip and eager to get home. He doesn't want to waste the time to go to the other fast food place just to get a drink. So, after going to the bathroom, Bob bends his principles a little—he hates giving the cheesy bastards any of his money—and he even suffers a small line in order to order something.

Bob thinks he is going to order a soda—he likes the dark kinds better than the clear kinds; and, please, don't even talk to him about diet—but at the last minute he decides to order a hot chocolate. It is a winter break he's going home on, not summer, and somehow a scorching Styrofoam cup in his hand, with the little plastic opening on the lid flying up to repeatedly hit him on the nose, seems to be just what he needs to remind him of the loving and safe haven that was his childhood home (not!) and to which he is now returning.

Bob arrives at the counter and lets the gangly teenager behind the register—the one wearing a silly paper hat and dressed in clashing shades of red and yellow—take his order.

"I'd like a hot chocolate with milk in it, please," Bob says politely to the young man—who, Bob can't help noticing, has a severe acne problem on his cheeks.

While the boy's right hand pushes the proper buttons on the electronic cash register, his left hand unconsciously moves up to rub his acne. Somehow the boy has sensed Bob looking at his dermatological imperfection and the boy is made self-conscious by it, although in an unconscious way. When the boy looks up from the register to tell Bob how much he owes for his hot chocolate, though, their eyes lock —and suddenly they both know they are thinking not about the hot chocolate, or how much it costs, but about the boy's acute case of acne and if he is ever going to get laid before it goes away in three or four years, if ever.

Hey, cut him some slack: Bob is a young man in college —and this is how he thinks about the world sometimes.

But, sadly, what is done is done. And before you can say "pop that zit," the young man cries out in anguish, focusing his rage on Bob.

The pimple-faced teenager lunges across the counter to grab Bob by the neck, but Bob steps back before he can be touched. Before the young man can strike again, however, the bulging veins in his temples pop open and the top of his head flies off like the peak of Mount Saint Helens. Bob can't believe what he is seeing. But hold on—it gets worse. Something is rumbling inside the crater that used to be the body of this young man, and before long, before Bob's horrified eyes, from out of the boy's carcass, wiggles a giant, human-size cockroach.

Bizarre enough, the roach is also wearing a paper hat and a red and yellow apron, but that is the only vestige of its prior incarnation as the acne-troubled young man. In its four upper limbs (Bob can't see the bottom two that it is presumably standing on behind the counter), the roach carries steaming cups of hot chocolate.

"Here, Bob," the creature hisses at him. "Here's your bloody hot chocolate."

Somehow Bob has the presence of mind not to run away. He digs deep in his pockets and finds that he does not have enough money for four cups—only for two.

Bob looks pleadingly at the roach.

"I'm sorry," Bob says, "I don't have what it takes."

Suddenly the roach drops all the cups at once. There is a strange smile that comes across its hideous face.

"We know, Bob," his roach server calls out, almost too playfully. And then it adds ominously, "Does the phrase 'fast food' mean anything to you?"

The roach's antennae rustle in the breeze from the ventilation fan over the grill—Bob's heart freezes in his throat.

Bob is thinking. Thinking fast. But not about food. He is thinking fast on his feet about survival. He searches for the correct phrase to appease the angry roach. He knows there must be one.

At last, Bob has it.

"To tell the truth, my friend," Bob proclaims as the creature climbs up onto the counter in front of him, "we should not exist."

The creature jumps onto Bob's torso, knocking him over. The creature's labial palps—the finger-like parts behind its mouth which test out the food and then scoop it into the mouth once proven safe—puncture the cavity of Bob's chest and then break through Bob's rib cage, searching for the grand organ in the depths of Piñata Bob.

"To tell the truth, my Bob," the roach spits out as it feasts quickly on Bob's heart, "as soon as we get rid of you, you won't."

Chapter 4:
Bob Becomes a Celebrity in an Alien Culture

B ob! Bob! Wake up, Bob, you're dreaming."
Bob comes to with a start. He is drenched in a pool of sweat and there is a terrible metallic taste in his mouth.

Standing over Bob with an air of concern are the nurse and Cock, who is peering at Bob from the edge of the elevated platform.

This dynamic duo is the first thing Bob sees when he opens his eyes and the last thing that he needs to see. To make matters worse, the nurse is unwittingly holding a bowl of hot chocolate near Bob's face.

In response, Bob shrieks as if there's no tomorrow.

Cock and the nurse back off, but Bob's screaming only increases in amplitude and longitude. Finally, Cock yells back, "Stop screaming, Bob! Do you want to lose your voice?! Imagine how horrible that would be for you!"

Somehow this practical message penetrates the fog around Bob's brain that is keeping the world of the dream alive, and Bob manages to quiet himself down.

Cock and the nurse exchange worried glances. The nurse suggests that it's time to hook Bob up to the IV to get his nerves back on track, but Cock is against the idea just yet. Cock is concerned that, in his present state, Bob may become dependent on the substance and Cock doesn't want another addiction—another long day's journey into cocoa night—on his record again.

For the time being, Cock tries another tactic.

"Bob, we've noticed you've been a little edgy since we brought you here. Perhaps we've tried to introduce you to society too quickly."

"I keep having terrible dreams," Bob says. At best, he seems on the verge of tears. At worst, madness.

"I can see that, Bob. We just need to get you acclimated to your new surroundings. You're going to be fine." Cock is talking a good game, but right now he's mostly in the convincing business, not the soothsaying business.

Bob looks at Cock blankly. He doesn't resist, he doesn't agree —in the words of political reporters, Bob neither confirms nor denies.

In light of Bob's nonresponse response, Cock continues, worried.

"We're going to try to get you to the program again today, but only after you've had all the chocolate you need. Clearly, the trip was harder on you than we realized and it seems some of your serotonin and endorphin levels were permanently depleted in transit along with your olfactory capacities. But don't worry, Bob. We're going to set that all right as rain before we venture out again."

"Excuse me," Bob says. Then he leans over the side of the bed and throws up. He wipes his mouth on the bedsheet. He looks at Cock with vacant eyes and says, "What were you saying about rain?"

Cock and the nurse are in a conference with the other roaches responsible for the Bring Bob Back project. They have been discussing the situation all morning, through rapid electromagnetic impulses between their antennae.

Yes, but how is he now? asks Charles the Larger. Charles is the scientist who first deciphered the precise Bob Coordinates.

He's fine. Sleeping peacefully, Cock reports.

The nurse elaborates: We felt it necessary to attach him to the IV. The intravenous cocoa seems to have stabilized not only his metabolism, but also his brain chemistry. Most significantly, his ependymal cells have regained their neural regeneration functions again and his dura mater is no longer dehydrated. Finally, a biopsy of the lateral ventricle shows that the toxoplasmocology has completely dissipated.

There is a silence after the nurse's medical report which is eventually broken by a regal roach in the corner.

That's all welcome news to be sure, nurse. Not to mention a remarkable recovery in such a short time—something for which you may take full credit. But the critical issue we're all concerned with is the danger of addiction.

This little speech comes from Pliny the Younger. Pliny is the scientist who first discovered a viable mathematical expression for the square root of negative one, thus removing it from the realm of imaginary numbers and into the realm of real numbers, which in turn enabled the reality of spacetime travel to occur. Understandably, Pliny is very precise about details. Especially safety details.

Again, as head of the project and as the roach closest to Bob, Cock answers.

At this point, Pliny, given Bob's reaction to our population and especially in light of his disturbing dreams and unstable emotional state, we thought it was absolutely worth the risk. We figure that once he comes to truly know us as a species, and grasps our inner beauty, his initial, ah, discomfort with our physical appearance will diminish, and then we'll be able to gradually wean him off the high dosages. Statistically, in the long run, he should be fine.

In other words, interrupts Deborah The Third, you don't know precisely what the long-term effects are, do you?

Cock looks at Deborah. She is the third in a remarkable line of healer roaches. There was a time—it seems like another lifetime ago—when the two were involved, but it was before Cock volunteered, against Deborah's wishes, for the Bring Bob Back Junket and had to undergo shrinkage. Now Cock and Deborah are more like cautious combatants. In fact, Cock thinks they have a relationship that rivals the bittersweet aftertaste of cocoa itself. But that is a different story and of little consequence to the Bob-related discussions at hand. So, instead of continuing this line of thought, Cock answers the question.

Yes, to get philosophical about it, Deborah, we never know for certain what the long-term effects of anything are.

Deborah picks up the double meaning—the uncertainty of their future mingled with the cosmic uncertainty of all futures—and Deborah's exoskeleton is atwitter with the nuances of Cock's statement. Oh, how Deborah misses batting antennae with dear ole Cock!

For the sake of Bob, Pliny interrupts this private/public discourse, can we please get back to the topic on the table?!

Deborah and Cock both wave their antennae at the group in a sign of apology. The group moves on.

What about traveling? Charles asks. Sure, Bob is swimming in the effects of the IV now—and happy as a spore, no doubt—but how are we going to get him on the road and keep him together?

Actually, Cock announces, the nurse has devised an ingenious plan.

The nurse reports proudly, drawing them a mental picture of her plan. I call it 'Cocoa à Go-Go,' she broadcasts.

With no further ado, the roaches agree to put the nurse's plan into action.

Bob (singing), Cock (whistling), and the nurse (rubbing its forelegs together and producing a type of melody from the stiff bristles hitting each other) are all riding up in the elevator, on their merry way to the surface of the Earth.

In the interim, Bob has undergone a miraculous recovery—his nerves are steady, his anxiety has retreated, and his health has never been better. To bolster the effects of the IV infusion, the nurse has devised a type of backpack for Bob to wear which contains the sacred liquid, complete with a sucking device positioned to the side of Bob's mouth. The entire contraption fits neatly under the Earth suit and all

Bob has to do to get a calming jolt is to turn his head to the side and suck at the straw-like device before him. At that point, the mood-altering cannabinoids will rush into his system, along with the opiates and other complex chemicals that make up chocolate, to produce a winsome pharmacological effect on the subsequent happy human.

"Feeling steady?" Cock asks as the elevator slows to its stop.

"Rock steady, Commander," a cheery Bob replies. "It's more than a feeling."

As the elevator doors open, the nurse—who is accompanying them for medical and safety reasons—waves an active set of antennae.

Bob notices and asks, "What's the good doctor saying now?"

Cock translates as they step out into the new day, "The nurse just asked me to remind you to take a sip if you begin to feel over-whelmed again."

"Can do, Captain. *No problema, Cucaracha Mama*," Bob asserts as he steps into his brave, new world. He's practically giddy—a case of *cocoa loco*, the nurse fears.

But Bob hasn't O.D.'ed. He's just high on life—a life buoyed by the magical effects of the cacao bean—and already he's bolting down the path on the way to their destination.

But this time, as the group makes its way to the program, Bob notices that glass-like walls have been put up on either side of the path.

"That wasn't there before," notes Bob.

"We had it put up in the meantime for you, Bob. It's sort of a temporary psychological barrier between you and our species as you get used to your new home."

"Well, thanks and all that," Bob says politely, "but now that I'm all tanked up, I don't feel so freaked out by you critters. But I do appreciate the sentiment and the effort. I surely do."

Even as he speaks, roaches come out from various deformed plant forms and, like curious beings everywhere, press their polysac-charide shells up against the transparent boundary, looking at Bob with curious insect eyes.

Bob takes a sip of cocoa and then like the Queen of England offers his loyal subjects a regal three-part wave. This seems to produce quite a delighted effect in the onlookers, and, as antennae everywhere start whipping around, even more roaches appear from the shadows to take a gander at Bob.

As they walk on and Bob continues his carefree I'm-the-marshal-of-the-parade activities, they come upon a small clearing. Rising above the heads of the roaches on the side of the path, Bob spies a type of roach motel—a high-rise structure with individual cubicles. The cockroaches are packed in tightly, one roach to a slot, and the front of the structure is completely open.

Bob stops and stares at the edifice complex, full of resting roaches. It's the first nonorganic object he's seen in roachland besides things associated specifically with him, such as the elevator and the hospitality house, and he's very curious.

"What in the world is that?" asks Bob. He's also a little unnerved, and so takes another hit from the straw.

"That is a meditation sanctuary," Cock explains.

"A mediation sanctuary?" asks Bob.

"Not 'mediation,'" corrects Cock, "'meditation.'"

"You meditate?" asks a surprised Bob.

"Of course we meditate. Everything in nature does. Only we've formalized it a bit more for collective effectiveness. You see, we only work a few hours a day—the couple hours before sunrise and the couple hours after sunset. Much of the rest of the time—time not spent maintaining relationships and procreative duties, that is—is spent in meditation. You probably can't tell, but there's an enormous amount of energy coming from that area right now."

"Believe me, I'm getting some kind of energy," Bob affirms, taking another sip from his straw. "But why are the rooms so small? They look so cramped."

"That's part of our way, Bob," Cock elucidates. "Our bodies

are incredible tactile receptors. We love physical feelings, we love sensation. To be touched on all sides at once—to experience sensation all around—is the most blissful feeling for us. Why, I'm getting exothermic chills now just thinking about it."

Bob can't tell if Cock is joking or not, but there does seem to be a kind of reverence in the tone of Cock's voice, so Bob concludes that it's all on the level.

"But don't you get claustrophobic?" For himself, Bob is not too keen about tight quarters.

"Not at all," Cock says. "We love the full body pressure. It produces feelings of well-being, safety, comfort, and home in us. We love it. Absolutely love it. Tight, dark places are the end of our rainbows."

"Different strokes," is all Bob can manage to say, and the group keeps strolling while Bob keeps sucking down the cocoa.

Shortly afterwards, the trio passes another clearing in the jungle. Here, on an elevated white dais—it reminds Bob vaguely of a giant aspirin tablet rising out of the ground—a huge cockroach is splayed out. Out of its anus, in neat little streams that shoot out between the cerci, come puffs of bluish-white gas.

"Holy Mary, Mother of God!" Bob gasps. And he's not even Catholic. "What the hell is that?!"

"Shhh!" Cock reproaches him. "It's a spot of elevated spirituality, Bob. You'll find out more about it in your training sessions. But suffice it to say for now that you are looking at a very holy activity."

Bob participates in his own holy activity and slurps down more hot chocolate. He also makes a mental note to find out more about this bizarre site—once they're at a safe distance, of course—and the group moves on.

The nurse signals to Cock, and Cock turns to Bob.

"Take it easy with that stuff, Bob. You don't want to run out before the program is over, do you?"

Before Bob can answer and defend his obsessive intake of

chocolate, they arrive in front of another elevator—this one being much larger than the one they came up on.

"What's this?" asks Bob.

"Service entrance," Cock says. "It's the back way to the program. We didn't want you to get mobbed."

Without further discussion, the three climb on board and descend into the dark, protective layers of the Earth's belly.

Bob is standing in the green room, out of his Earth suit and naked, waiting for Cock to bring him some clothes. At last, Cock enters on a motorized platform.

"There you are!" Bob says, relieved. "Where have you been?"

"Going over the program schedule. But the real question is where have *you* been? The production assistant has been looking all over for you," Cock responds. "What are you still doing in here?"

"The nurse took away my suit," Bob answers. "I've been waiting for you."

"Oh, I see. A little shy? Okay, I'm here, so let's go."

Bob stands buck naked with his arms akimbo.

"Don't you think I'm missing something?"

Cock looks him over from head to toe, pausing ever so slightly at Bob's midsection.

"Oh, of course," Cock laughs. "How could I have been so silly."

Cock wiggles the ever-helpful antennae.

Instantly, two cockroaches enter with trays of body paint.

"No, not makeup!" Bob yells. "Get them out of here!"

Cock signals to the new arrivals to leave, as Bob continues, "Clothes. I need some clothes."

"Clothes?" asks a confused Cock. "The temperature is perfect for a human."

"It's not about temperature!" Bob states emphatically.

"Then what's it about?" Cock wants to know.

"It's about—oh, never mind." Bob gives up. "Just get me something to wear."

"Hold on," Cock says. "This is unexpected. We wanted to show our society a human in his natural state."

"Living in a world of roaches is hardly my natural state!"

"I mean your 'birthday suit' natural state."

"Ix-nay on the aked-nay!" Bob yells. "I didn't drag my private penis across millions of miles of spacetime to show it to a bunch of 'I am Curious Yellow' roaches!"

"Okay, calm down. I'll see what I can do."

Then Cock mumbles to himself in a stage whisper as he rolls out the door, "Geez, so touchy!"

Bob sits down in front of a wall of lighted mirrors. He puts his head in his hands and looks up occasionally at the face staring back at him. But he's having a difficult time looking at himself too closely. His own image reminds him of how much he misses the beauty —the grace, the elegant majesty—of the human form. He can barely stand to look at his own hands, let alone his features. For when Bob looks at his hands, he no longer sees his own hands—instead, he sees the last pair of human hands left surviving. His own body hardly even belongs to him anymore. Instead, it belongs to a memory of a genus, a taxonomy, a category that no longer exists—except here in this one exceptional and final case. At times like this, left alone in front of a mirror, Bob can hardly stand the heartache of it all. The singularity of his humanity oppresses him. He is but one human reflected back on himself. A singular instance—one Bob, indivisible—unbroken and irreparable all at once.

Suddenly, saving Bob from this lonesome train of thought, which is exactly the kind of thing he thinks when he's alone, Cock rolls in with a sartorial announcement.

"You're in luck, Bob. The curators at the human museum had some things in your size."

Behind Cock are two cockroaches who wheel in a coatrack

filled with costumes from all times in human history. Cock watches with amusement as Bob examines several of the outfits. First Bob holds up the animal wraps of the cave dweller. Next it is the cloth drapes of the Roman statesman. Then it is the flowing cape of the medieval alchemist. Finally, for his own warped reasons, Bob settles on a historically peculiar outfit: a powder-blue leisure suit complemented by a colorful Hawaiian shirt.

"Bitchin'," Bob says to his bemused image.

"Come on, Dann-o," Cock warns. "You're on in five."

Cock heads out toward the stage and Bob follows, snapping his cuffs into place.

So there they are, the three of them—Bob, Little Cock, and the host, a full-size roach holding index cards—all sitting in a row on a stage.

Bob himself is in a tiny baby blue spotlight—a nice compliment to his suit choice, he thinks—but everything else remains dark and cozy.

Hey, I'm on a talk show, realizes Bob.

"It's a *think* show," corrects Cock. "You and I are the only ones who will be talking, after all."

Sitting and corrected, a blue Bob nods and takes in the environment.

There is a floor-to-ceiling transparent wall in front of them —it looks like the glass boundary that sectioned off the jungle path —and in the dim light Bob can see on the other side that the audience chamber is filling up with cockroaches.

Bob sits there, next to a table holding his ever-present cup of hot chocolate, and watches the audience tank crowd-up with roaches crawling on top of each other, making piles and piles of writhing, twitching bodies.

Quickly, Bob takes a sip of his drink.

Suddenly, watching this seething mass of roachness, Bob has

an insight not only into his own plight, but into little Cock's as well. Bob whispers to Cock as the host prepares to introduce them.

"Cock, are you always going to be that size?"

Cock is surprised by the question; it's the first time Bob has shown any genuine interest in his guide. Flattered, Cock answers readily.

"Yes, Bob. It's from the spacetime travel. I had to be made smaller to survive the round-trip journey. It was an enormous stress on my metabolism—I'll be lucky to live out my normal life span."

"How long is that?" Bob wonders.

"About seven and a half years, give or take a few months."

"Can't they bring you back to your normal size?"

"Oh, no. I wouldn't survive the transformation again. Quanta are pliable, but not indefinitely."

"But what about your personal life?"

"What do you mean, Bob?"

"You know. Mating. Sex."

"Oh, I hardly think I'll be knocking antennae with anyone again. Unless a certain someone chooses to give up a promising career to lead the refugee life of a diminutive roach, and then undergoes the shrinkage transformation for purely elective reasons. But, frankly, just between us, I don't see that happening."

"So you're going to be alone?"

"No, little buddy," Cock says with wry humor, "not as long as you're around, I won't."

For a moment Bob thinks Cock is making some kind of bizarre inter-species sexual proposition, but then Bob realizes that Cock is merely comparing their similar situations as outsiders in a culture—a situation that does, Bob realizes for the first time, inexorably bind them together.

Before Bob can offer any thoughts on their odd family-style relationship, the host thinks to Cock in their native language.

Cock announces, "They're almost ready for us, Bob. Now just

sit there quietly until I start to translate questions for you."

Bob nods his head—and then stares in astonishment as two cockroaches prance onto the stage wearing brightly colored paper hats.

"Oh, you're going to love this," whispers Cock. "They're our best singers."

"Singers?!" asks Bob incredulously. "With no voice boxes, what could they possibly sing?!"

"Well, technically, it's called stridulation—the rubbing together of two body parts. But believe me, it's heavenly."

Bob prepares for the worst as the cockroaches begin to make their music together. Once in the center of the stage, each roach stiffens its legs, pumps up its abdomen, and begins to vibrate. Along the edges of the pronotum—the armor-like shoulders just behind the head —are small nail-like ridges called striae. The thick outer edge of the forewing also contains striae, and, like a guitar pick, the pronotum striae strum up and down the striae of the forewing. This produces a sonification that is, more or less, similar in nature to a beauteous pastoral melody—and, before long, it's a regular hootenanny. The audience roaches are trembling in exultant ecstasy, and even Bob can't help tapping a toe or two. Of course, Bob keeps it all in check with gulps from his travel cup, but, given the circumstances, and his lack of stimulating social activities, who could blame him?

After the duet comes to a halt, and the mass of antennae whipping dies down a bit, the host turns to Cock who in turn turns to Bob. Cock then speaks in an officious voice.

"Our society wishes to express its enormous gratitude to you, Bob, for coming on this difficult journey away from your homeland and loved ones to help us in an altruistic manner. Our species is forever indebted to your courage and your selflessness in coming."

Bob is quite touched by these sentiments and he quickly wipes what would have been a tear from his eye had he given it the chance to fully develop.

Bob stares at the masses behind the glass wall and responds

earnestly, "Thank you for your kind words. Even though the journey has been difficult, I am thankful for your kind hospitality and for the opportunity to learn of things I never even dreamed were imaginable."

Because the audience behind the glass wall is more than five feet away from Bob, and thus out of antennae shot of Bob's weak brainwaves, Cock must translate Bob's response. Cock does, and it brings a great rustle of enthusiasm from the crowd.

Warming up to his newfound popularity, Bob offers to take specific questions about his own world. The host readily agrees to this suggestion and opens up questions to the audience.

Cock translates the first question for Bob, saying, "The couple from Palenque want to know why you aren't green. They thought that all humans were green."

Bob is surprised at the question, but answers it as best he can.

"Perhaps you had us confused with the dinosaurs, who we also, erroneously, thought to be green. But, no, I don't know of any humans who were green in skin tone. The majority of humans were brown or black in skin tone, with another large percentage being pinkish or cream-colored. Skin tone, like hair color and eye color, showed a great variety around the globe and the combinations, not to mention subtle variations, on the dominant themes were almost limitless."

This answer pleases the couple from Palenque very much and Bob is happy to have been so informative. In fact, Bob always felt that his true calling was as an expert—something more profound than being a "computer" expert, which he thought of as being only slightly better sometimes than being a "toaster" expert—Bob just never knew what it was he could rightly be an expert in. Now he knows. As the only surviving member of a lost civilization that ended millions of years ago, Bob is suddenly the most knowledgeable guy in town on all things considered human.

But, before Bob can get too full of himself, Cock translates the next question, "The mystic from Bhutan would like to know,

Bob, what you believe the human soul to be made of—paper or plastic?"

"Definitely paper," Bob responds deadpan.

Cock translates a follow-up question, "The mystic from Bhutan would like to know your reasoning for your answer."

Bob takes a big swig from his travel cup and launches into it as best he can.

"Paper is biodegradable," Bob explains, "and plastic is likely to hang around for thousands, perhaps even millions, of years. So, given that the human species lasted only several thousand years and not several million years, I can answer resolutely that the human soul was made of paper, and not plastic. For, if the human soul had been truly made of plastic, certainly our species would have lasted as long as plastic does. Since it didn't, I can only conclude that our souls were made out of a flimsy substance such as paper. The evidence and my logical construction of it seem irrefutable."

Cock translates once again and then responds to Bob, "Although you are considered a spiritual ignoramus, the mystic from Bhutan thanks you for your considered opinions."

And so this is how it goes—back and forth, question and answer, cockroach and human—for several hours, until Bob's stamina runs out and it's time for him to return to the hospitality house to begin his strenuous training sessions in preparation for the journey to The Great Temple of the Arc, which houses the mysterious Chamber of the Second Sun.

Unexpected Memory Interruption #4:
Pining for the Beauty of Movie Stars

B ob is walking along—alone—in a tangle of over-lapping vines and enormous stalks. There's a good reason he's alone: he's the last human on Earth. And he is making his solitary way through a dense, green tropical jungle. He has a machete and a hat and a pair of good, solid jungle boots, but otherwise he is naked. And he is hacking his way forward, relentlessly.

At last, Bob comes upon a clearing. He pokes his head through the underbrush and spies a disturbing scene: seven huge cockroaches, standing in a semicircle, are gathered around a giant, life-size television intently watching its contents. Inside the television, however, are dozens of real-life movie stars—Bob recognizes some of the more famous ones—standing and chatting in the midst of what looks like an elegant cocktail party. It's as if the TV is a house (or a stage), but all the inhabitants (or actors) don't know they are really inside a gigantic television set.

Bob, though, is less concerned with the oversized dimensions and logic of it all. He's simply ecstatic that he's found other humans. He is so very relieved not to be the last one. The enormity of it all was starting to bug him.

Suddenly, Bob can no longer stand to be separated from his kind. He bursts onto the scene and startles the placid roaches. Before they can react, Bob runs around to the back of the huge box trying to find a door, or a cable, or any kind of opening at all—trying to find some way to get in, in order to be with his people.

The roaches seem very upset by Bob's presence—or maybe it's that they're upset by his attempts to enter the

TV. For their part, the glamorous folks inside the box don't seem to be aware of Bob any more than they are of the roaches. The beautiful people continue, uninterrupted, their chatting, their sipping, their gracious laughter.

In the meantime, the roaches are chasing Bob around the television set. He swipes his machete at them, doing little damage except to lob off the foreleg of the nearest one. Bob is astounded, though, as the missing limb immediately grows back, smaller but intact. Bob runs faster.

But, of course, it is to no avail.

Eventually, the roaches surround him in front of the set. Bob has only the roaches before him and the TV behind him. The roaches close in. Desperate to escape, Bob turns around and dives headfirst through the TV screen and into the movie star party.

It is as if he has entered another world.

Bob picks himself up carefully from the shards and checks to see that he is not too badly cut. He isn't. Then he turns around to see if the roaches have followed him, but they remain—in a haze—on the other side of the screen, a snowy curtain that they can't penetrate.

Safe, for the moment, Bob takes off his hat and uses it as a modest cover to shield his privates. He hides behind a potted palm and wonders what to do about his nakedness.

Within moments, a waiter in a tuxedo and waist apron walks by holding with both hands a huge tray of empty glasses. Bob scurries behind the man, unnoticed, and unties the apron. Bob then fashions it like a kilt, puts his hat firmly back on his head, and strides confidently into the party.

But the party that Bob joins is markedly different from the one that Bob first viewed from the clearing.

For what at first glance was a party full of beautiful, exciting people in glamorous, shimmering outfits is now a party full of beautiful, exciting people in exquisite, chiseled bare bodies. Oh, the accessories are still there: the expensive watches, the silk cummerbunds, the matching bow ties, the trendy sunglasses, the evening gloves, the strings of pearls, the slippers, the wingtips, the French cuffs, the fine Italian leather belts. But their bodies—their beautiful, luscious, curvaceous, supple, slinky, lanky, gracious, sexy, unanimously enticing bodies—are all shining naked, beholden in the glory God gave them.

But the color of the bodies? All pale as ash, a ghostly pallor washed over them all.

Bob is astounded. He has never seen so much perfect beauty in one place before. It's as if all the Greek and Roman statues from the Met gathered en masse in glorious animated form for the most enticing fund-raiser of all time. Bob's eyes cannot drink in fast enough the wanton exhibition of unadulterated human form. He wanders aimlessly—mesmerized—among the party guests, soaking up the rhapsody of the corporeal feast. At last, visually satiated, Bob sinks to the floor and cries out in religious ecstasy, thanking the heavens for the beauty and the eminence of the human body.

But in doing this, Bob breaks the enchantment. For when he raises his head from the floor, he sees that—where before he had been invisible—now everyone is staring at him. And clearly he does not belong. They all gather around Bob in a great mob, saying nothing, but speaking their disgust at him in volumes.

Bob stands and starts to explain what has happened to him and why he is wearing his ridiculous outfit, but he finds he can't speak. He reaches out to touch someone, any-one, but they shrink back from him as if he were a leper.

Bob turns quickly and catches a handsome man off

guard. Bob reaches out and grabs the man's hand, but the hand and entire arm stiffen at a right angle and break off in Bob's grasp. The handsome man is made of fragile plaster and he cracks and crumbles before Bob like day-old dust.

And there, inside—where the man's viscera ought to be—are hoards and hoards of teaming, wriggling, stinking, twitching domestic American cockroaches.

Everyone shrieks, including Bob. The cockroaches dash everywhere, causing a mass stampede. But the movie stars are trapped in the lugubrious nature of their party and their world and they all end up stuck, just running in place, like in a bad dream.

Bob is pushing past them as best he can, bumping up against them, and every person he touches cracks and crumbles, their fragile plaster outline breaking, and their innards of cockroaches joining the mess already loose.

Bob makes his way back toward the screen where he crashed in, but there blocking his way is a line of seven naked waiters, complete with towels tucked in waist belts and trays raised on high like shields. Bob runs past them quickly, smashing his fist through each of their washboard abs and he watches the same horrifying spectacle unravel seven times: the plaster bodies crack and crumble and the teaming hoards of cockroaches pour out from what is left of them.

Before he blacks out from disgust, Bob takes a running leap and flies headfirst back through the smashed screen through which he first entered this hideous world.

On the other side, the seven huge cockroaches are waiting patiently for Bob.

First, though, Bob turns around to see if the horrors of the TV world have followed him. But, no, like the huge roaches who could not follow Bob inside in the first place, these human and domestic pest cockroaches are trapped inside their world, too. Bob watches in horrified amazement as the tiny roaches crawl up on the inside of the screen, eventually obscuring all the screaming humans racing toward the screen to get out. Occasionally, a movie star runs smack into the glass, bursting himself open like a bug on a windshield and releasing into the TV world thousands more internal pests.

Almost unable to tear himself from the gory site, Bob at last turns to face his row of roaches, here in the jungle.

Bob takes a brave step forward to meet his fate.

The roaches encircle him.

Unnerved, Bob automatically grabs for his machete, but quickly realizes he left it inside the TV. Now without arms, Bob resorts to his arms. Instinctively, Bob pushes the nearest roach away from him with a hard shove. But instead of stumbling backward, as Bob expects, the creature cracks and crumbles. It, too, is made of fragile plaster—just like the humans. But, unlike the humans, inside there is no phalanx of roaches.

Instead, inside this huge roach is a blue-skinned human-like being with eight arms and light emanating from its translucent body. The humanoid figure is adorned with golden spangles and bracelets, armbands, and necklaces of sandalwood. It is like a beautiful Hindu god, and it hovers there, cross-legged, above the ground shimmering in the light, gently swaying in the sensuous movements of the Odissi style of dance.

The other roaches now stand in a row before Bob, who is terrified and calm all at the same time. On impulse, Bob runs past the row of upright cockroaches strumming his hand across their exposed abdomens, like trailing a stick against a picket fence. As his hand touches each roach belly, the creature cracks and crumbles, and there inside each of

them is a Hindu god, each in a different pastel color—
refractions of natural light—each with many sets of arms,
each adorned in gold and ornaments, each hovering above
the Earth, each shining with the light of peace and well-being,
the luminous outlines of their exquisite forms suggesting
the soft curves of ancient temple sculptures.

The beings hover around Bob in a semicircle and out-
stretch their many, many arms toward him. He feels it. He
feels their goodness. Their eternal, etheric intentions hit him
like a searing crack of lightning.

At long last, Bob understands. And then he weeps
without end.

Chapter 5:
Bob Undergoes Training for the Trip of Mysteries

When Cock enters the underground training facility where Bob
has been transferred, a cozy site awaits.

Bob is running on a type of mechanized treadmill—building
his strength, his lung capacity, and the calluses on his bare feet—
while the nurse monitors his progress and matches his gait on a similar
contraption. The two run in place, side by side—Bob vertical, the
nurse horizontal—but the nurse, by far, is outstripping him, stride
for stride. If Bob thought that cockroaches were fast when they were
toe-size, he is shocked to discover the proportionate speed ratio of
these mega-sized ones.

In addition to this charming, trotting *pas de deux*, Cock notices
that Bob is wearing an intriguing outfit.

For, having made fans of the human museum curators during
his celebrity moment, Bob was allowed to keep some of the costumes
he particularly admired. As a result, Bob now sports a bizarre little
wardrobe while at the training facility—he's a Roman emperor one
day, Greek foot soldier the next, followed by a south-side Juke Joint
Johnny. One day, Bob even opted for a smart little candy striper's
jumper, but the notion seemed to be completely lost on the nurse.

Currently, Bob is modeling an early fashion basic from the
Neander Valley in prehistoric Germany—the bearskin loincloth. He
wears it with no small degree of irony—irony which is further bol-
stered by the knowledge that all the clothes he took for propriety's

sake were made by the roaches from various plant fibers and based on images found in badly tattered books. In other words, there's not a bear hair to be found—in the room or on the planet.

So this is how Cock finds Bob: sweating under the cover of his fake-fur loincloth and the repetitions of his labor, a challenging regimen instituted, in part, to keep off the weight that Bob would otherwise be gaining from his massive consumption of chocolate.

For Bob's part, he finds himself in a training facility that, even though it seems especially built for him and the specifics of human anatomy, doesn't compensate for its sterility, spookiness, and general lack of warmth.

It's too much like a mental ward. Or a military compound. And Bob has an aversion to guns. It goes along with his congenital aversion to authority. And his aversion to the lies that sustain military culture as well as the brute force and destruction that is its end. It wasn't for nothing that back in his subterranean glory days—before surfacing above ground and getting the job with SIMS, Inc.—Bob hacked into the Pentagon Web site and substituted "Have a bloody day!" on its not-so-welcoming home page. He was never caught, although he never tried it again, either.

But here he is—now—a little soldier of the future, training for some maneuver whose specifics and end he cannot conceive...or so easily manipulate.

It is precisely because Bob has such little insight into the nature of his journey that Cock has come to relieve him again of his physical training—which is in preparation of their journey to The Great Temple of the Arc—and supplement his understanding with more knowledge about what lies ahead.

"Hello, Bob!" Cock calls out.

Happy to see his chum and mentor, Bob is agreeably shaken from his thoughts.

"Is it philosophy time already?" Bob smiles.

"I'm afraid so, my larva pupil."

"That's Mr. Pupa to you, my bug-eyed friend."

Bob likes playing with Cock, and teasing Cock, too—it sure beats being pontificated at by the little critter when Cock gets on a moral spouting spree. Besides, at this point, language is about all Bob has left of his world—that and memories and dreams—and he is more grateful to Cock than he himself realizes for being able to share this last remaining invention of the *Homo sapiens*.

For Bob has been the witness to this, if nothing else: Even after human technology ends and human bodies decompose, human language remains. Just another confirmation, Bob decides, of why it was more important to write books than build bombs. Why, the cave paintings in France alone, with their human and animal figures painted in shades of ocher and red hematite and hues of charcoal and ash, have more humanity in them than all the military contractors in Orange County.

And, while he's thinking about those Neanderthal homes, Bob realizes that a bear skull placed reverently on a stone altar in the dark recesses of a cave says more about what it is to experience the divine than all the cathedrals in Rome built off the labor of *de facto* slaves and the wealth siphoned off of peasants.

In short, from the perspective of the future, which is the literal perspective of boundless hindsight, Bob knows everything and nothing about his world; and he has no idea what insight he might be able to give these advanced creatures who are so curious about the ones who came before.

The universe is 13 billion years old. The Earth, 4.6 billion. Humanoid bipedal creatures are maybe three or four million years old, at the outer limits. *Homo sapiens* ("wise humans")—the direct descendants of *Homo habilis* ("skillful humans") and *Home erectus* ("upright humans")—are about 40,000 years old. Such short, short time spans given the totality of what has come before. How can humans know anything given such a comparative lack of existence? Who then has pondered long enough on the human condition to know enough about it to say anything of worth?

Who, indeed. The cockroaches have—those wise scions of the most dominant form of visible life on the planet: insects, the ubiquitous creatures who appear in the fossil record some 400 million years before humans. And now Bob is about to hear all about it—straight from the roach's mouth.

"So," Cock begins. But Cock doesn't follow this opener with anything. It remains hanging in the air, a verbal throat clearing.

Bob and Cock are sitting in a sterile little room off the main training room. Big vats of dehydrated cocoa line the walls. It's a type of underground grain elevator for cockroaches—cockroaches who have made a virtual career out of preparing for, dealing with, and surviving catastrophes. Adult cockroaches can sometimes be found admonishing their growing larvae, "Store what you eat and eat what you store." It's good advice, guidance that the entire civilization takes to heart. So, it is in this space of sustenance precaution that Cock conducts instructive dialogues with Bob about the mystery of Sun worshipping, the very mystery that Bob is here to help solve.

To help Bob get up to speed on the subject, Cock has already gone over some of the basics of Sun science and Sun activity, including sunspots (gas on the Sun's surface of lower temperature occurring in 11-year cycles), solar flares (gigantic, million-mile torches released through weaknesses in the Sun's magnetic fields), prominences (giant arcs of flame curving out into space and then back toward the Sun), spicules (explosions from the interior of the Sun which send out the "solar wind"), and the solar wind itself (streams of charged particles rushing through space and affecting the Earth's magnetic fields).

Bob has already passed a quiz on all this and can also recite from memory that the Sun is a typical medium-sized yellow star, a luminous ball of gas powered by the chain fusion reaction of hydrogen nuclei at its core. Bob now knows that the Sun—which is currently about halfway through its life cycle—has enough energy in its core to burn 10 billion years before the depletion of hydrogen and the ensuing series of chemical reactions transform it into a white dwarf. In a universe of 125 billion galaxies (and counting), with each galaxy containing billions and billions of stars, Bob's Sun and its life cycle stand out as "unique" in no way whatsoever. Bob knows this because he answered a bonus question about it correctly. And Bob got another of the bonus questions correct when he answered that the *aurora borealis* (or the northern lights) is produced by the collision of the Earth's air molecules with the solar wind.

Having thus successfully completed the basics of Sun science, Cock then moved on from the workings of the Sun to its impact on the Earth. This section in Bob's notes is appropriately entitled, "The Sun: The Creator and Sustainer of All Life on Earth." (It's evident that Bob is a good note taker. It's part of what makes him a good programmer. He listens. He takes notes. He studies the notes. He understands. It's a simple, logical process, one that he has followed to success through three increasingly rewarding jobs and, now, two periods of spacetime.)

Bob's notes also contain more background on how climate patterns on the Sun (specifically storms, such as sunspots and solar flares) can dramatically affect climate patterns on Earth, including causing radio and electrical interference. This is part of the whole Sun-Earth connection, a concept that is relentlessly being drilled into Bob's consciousness in the hopes that he will now be able to recognize even the most oblique human references to it.

But, of course, the main topic of discussion in this session centered on photosynthesis. By the end of the lesson Bob was able to repeat, believe, and understand that "all life on Earth is a complex chemical reaction ultimately dependent upon the storing of solar energy by plants."

This, of course, was true merely for the geological era that Bob and other contemporaneous species came from. However, millions of years ago, before plants evolved, there still existed life on Earth, but it was life that didn't depend on plants. That is, before the early plants came the early animals (simple creatures of the sea who eventually developed shells and skeletons) and before the early sea animals were bacteria (including late forms such as mitochondria and chloroplasts and early forms such as single-cell microorganisms). In fact, ever since bacterial cells first appeared—3.5 billion years ago—they have been the dominant form of life on Earth, cleverly inventing all of life's essential biotechnolgies along the way: fermentation, photosynthesis, respiration, sensing devices and motion, DNA repair, the trading of genes, and nucleated cells.

The first type of photosynthesis that bacteria invented looked nothing like what Bob was vaguely familiar with in his former world of green plants. Instead, that first incarnation of photosynthesis had the bacteria taking not water as their source of hydrogen, but instead hydrogen sulfide (which was a plentiful gas spewed out by the many active volcanoes on the Earth at the time). The bacteria took the hydrogen sulfide and then, using solar energy, combined it with carbon dioxide from the air to make the carbohydrate compounds necessary for life. In this first version of photosynthesis, no oxygen was released.

In the second incarnation of photosynthesis, a new type of bacteria evolved (the ancestors of what would become blue-green algae) which now took its source of hydrogen from the abundant oceans of the Earth and then combined it—again, using solar energy—with carbon dioxide from the air to form complex carbohydrates. But this time, the waste product of this process was not excess sulfur compounds, as in the previous process, but excess oxygen. A new technology had been born—oxygenic photosynthesis—and the evolutionary road was thus paved for oxygen-breathing organisms.

This new form of bacterial photosynthesis was spectacularly successful. Actually, too successful. For, as a result, too much oxygen built up in the air, which at the time (approximately two billion years ago) eventually produced a toxic atmospheric hazard of catastrophic proportions. But the bacteria weren't done inventing life just yet. No, the planet would not become engulfed in combustible outbreaks, as it would have had the oxygen build-up continued unchecked. Instead, evolution took a gigantic leap forward, and certain types of bacteria appeared which survived via a new biotechnology—what humans now call respiration.

At last, the wonder of wonders had happened: the creatures had reconstituted themselves to actually require the very substance that before had been toxic to them—oxygen. Bacteria breathed, and the fragile but tenacious web of life breathed along with them a collective sigh of relief.

Once respiration existed, an explosion of life-form diversity ensued. For, while it took bacteria almost two billion years to invent respiration, it took only about half that time for the first animals to appear; and after the first sea animals appeared, it took only about half that time again for flowering plants, land animals, and the first primates to appear. Life was exploding at a dizzying geo-historical rate.

However, all this manifold unfolding of life came to an abrupt halt when the most rambunctious of primates brought to morbid fruition their misadventures with atomic fission.

This part of the story Bob not only knows, but has experienced, in part, firsthand. He knows the history of the race for The Bomb—a weapon of practically unlimited destruction—and the consequences of that ill-fated contest. He knows about the A-bomb that atomized Hiroshima and the H-bomb that hindered hope and human futures. Bob knows these things; in fact, he has recently jettisoned away from the doomed fetters of these things, and so Cock did not dwell on this historical interlude, except to point out the dramatic effects of mass nuclear detonation on the atmosphere.

In other words, Cock quickly and succinctly—much to Bob's relief—reviewed how the worldwide explosions of nuclear devices and the failure of nuclear reactors produced a massive release of ozone-destroying chemicals into the atmosphere (in addition to destroying lots of life directly through explosions and radiation poisoning, of course). Moreover, Cock explained how more ozone-depleting chemicals were produced by the *consequences* of the nuclear explosions, particularly the massive fulminations of volcanoes and the release of industrial chemical reserves.

("But why the sudden multiplication of volcanoes?" Bob had asked. Cock had to explain how the underground detonations created great fissures in the Earth's surface allowing gases and magma to escape, and also how the weakened magnetic field allowed the pressures from the Earth's core to erupt through the Earth's surface.)

Within the blink of an eye, millions of cubic tons of dangerous gases were released into the atmosphere as a result of the widespread nuclear blasts and ensuing ecological disasters. Cock reels off the names like the attendance list at some hideous family reunion: methyl bromide, carbon tetrachloride, methyl chloroform, various halons and chlorines, hydrochloric acid, chlorine monoxide, sulfuric acid, and the big rooster of them all, chlorofluorocarbons. All these compounds broke down in the stratosphere and yielded chemical by-products that destroyed ozone.

At this point, Cock reminded Bob that ozone is a molecule consisting of three atoms of oxygen instead of the more common two. These ozone molecules had collected over time to form the ozone layer—a protective blanket at the outer edge of the stratosphere, 15 to 30 miles above the Earth's surface—which prevented most of the Sun's harmful radiation from reaching the Earth. The ozone layer was a big custodial umbrella in the sky, which was needed to safeguard animal and plant tissue from the dangerous effects of solar ultraviolet radiation.

When the ozone layer was destroyed, the Sun's radiation fell full force on the Earth, and the few remaining plants, animals, and insects who had not already died from the radiation poisoning produced by the nuclear catastrophes on Earth (the humans had long since perished), quickly were leveled by the additional poisons raining in from the sky.

As Cock had mentioned to Bob in his kitchen, the only creatures surviving after the ozone disappeared were the cockroaches, along with certain viruses and bacteria. It was left to these straggling species to reconstitute the entire web of life on the planet. It was an enormous task set before them, but one which they readily and immediately began to address. And the way they did it was by inventing the third incarnation of photosynthesis—perhaps better called radiasynthesis.

"So," Cock repeats as Bob shifts uncomfortably in his chair. "Shall we continue where we left off?"

Without waiting for an answer, Cock begins Bob's daily lesson, explaining the third evolution in photosynthesis. This is the main evolutionary process with which cockroaches, bacteria, and plants are now intimately involved, and by which they are transforming the chemical composition of the Earth—particularly, what's left of its biosphere. Bob listens carefully, his cup of hot cocoa ever present, hovering near pursed lips.

"As the bacteria of yesteryear showed us," Cock begins, "the thing to do now was to absorb the poison that was all around us— that is, the radiation that had destroyed nearly everything in its path —and turn it into the very substance we required to propagate life. Within a few hundred generations—cockroaches, viruses, and bacteria all reproduce very quickly, you know—we had successfully transformed our primary intake needs from compounds of hydrogen, carbon, and oxygen to radiation. And, as a waste product, instead of producing greenhouse gases such as methane and carbon monoxide, we began excreting fumes comprised primarily of ozone."

"How hideous," Bob gasps.

"No," Cock answers, "to the contrary: that's the elegance of life."

"So that creature farting on the dais..." Bob trails off his line of thought as the image from the path comes back to haunt him.

"Yes," answers Cock, "in the ecstatic thralls of ridding the Earth of radiation by absorbing it and producing what the Earth needs most by excreting ozone. A lot of our most sacred ceremonies have to do with the production of ozone. You caught a glimpse of just one of those rituals."

"Passing gas is holy?" Bob can't help scoffing. "And you thought *my* world was depraved."

Cock ignores Bob's scatological protestations and continues undaunted, "Our physical bodies are now finely-tuned systems successfully evolved to absorb radiation and use it to fuel our metabolic processes, and then excrete from it the exact waste product that the Earth needs most to attain a full biodiversity of life again: ozone."

"Let me get this right," Bob tries again. "You're sucking up the radiation like a fine bouillabaisse in one end and farting out ozone from the other?"

"I think there are more poetic ways to describe it—not to mention other ways that are more anatomically accurate—but, more or less, yes."

"How disgusting."

Bob gulps more cocoa.

"Not at all. Think of it as nature's ingenious method of rebuilding the web of life."

Bob is yet to be convinced.

"But how is it all going to end for you?" he wonders.

Given the rank demise of his own kind, Bob is very curious about the long-term fate of his hosts.

"As a species, not so good," Cock admits. "We're like the ultimate physicians who have taken the ultimate Hippocratic Oath—the first impulse is to help where possible and the second is to at least cause no harm where not. The final oath is to try to alleviate the need for one's services in the first place. We're in the business of making ourselves obsolete."

"What do you mean?" Bob asks.

"As we thrive as a species, we will eventually take over the entire planet. And, like all rapidly expanding living systems, we will produce enormous amounts of waste. In our case, ozone. In time, as our gaseous wastes collect and accumulate in the stratosphere, we will have completely rebuilt the ozone layer. This will, in turn, divert the Sun's radiation, and allow new life-forms to evolve. However, the ozone layer will be deflecting the very radiation we need to survive. Therefore, in time, our very success at life will create the very change in the atmosphere that cuts us off from what we need most to survive: radiation."

Bob's brow furrows.

"But," he says, "if you mutated to absorb enormous amounts of radiation and survived, why couldn't you mutate back to *not* need it?"

"The world doesn't evolve backwards, Bob. The nature of life progresses *forward*. In order to survive, we would have to mutate into something new, yet again. But we've discovered that our genetic code has been tapped out. We're a long-standing model, but eventually we will be retired and something more flexible, and more *needed*, will evolve to fill the gap we will leave."

"You mean, you have a planned obsolescence?"

"Yes, and we don't even come with a money-back guarantee."

"How can you joke of all this?" Bob asks.

"Life is not anything, if it's not funny," Cock assures.

"I'm amazed at your lack of will to live."

"Oh, we have plenty of will to live," Cock insists. "It's just that that will extends beyond our own shortsighted, self-serving needs and reaches to every corner of the planet. While we're perfectly happy with our own species and our own culture, we viscerally understand that the lack of biodiversity is a great loss to the planet. We're honored to help change that."

"Somehow, your lack of indignation at your own demise seems

less than admirable," Bob mutters.

"Less than admirable?!" Cock cries. "To refuse to pursue merely our own selfish interests? To refuse to be indifferent to any greater good? Hardly, Bob. This is the genetic imperative: for all organisms to pursue communal interests, always aware of the greater good and the long-term future. We abide by it. This maxim is at the heart of natural law. To the contrary, what would you call the behavior of your species, you mutant creatures of selfish genes, you hideous cankers who tottered ever so briefly on the cusp of monsterhood only to plunge forward into it full force? It took three billion years for the Earth to develop a stable oxygen-sufficient atmosphere, and an ozone layer that could shelter the development of life on the planet's surface. You humans blasted it away practically in the blink of an eye. How 'admirable' is that, Bob?"

"If you remember correctly, Cock, you whisked me away from all that before it happened."

Bob is certainly not going to take the wrap for something he wasn't even around to see.

"Before it happened *then*. But not before it happened *now*. That is merely a technical point of spacetime travel that you're making, Bob. But the moral point is that you and your kind destroyed something in an instant that had taken billions of years to evolve— the biosphere. And now that the experiment that was humanity is at last—thankfully—over, we are slowly rebuilding that biosphere."

"But it will eventually mean your own demise!"

Bob simply cannot comprehend the cockroach predilection for allegiance to the big picture, or the so-called web of life, over the continuation of the specific species.

"There are much worse things, Bob," Cock notes sadly. "Such as to cause the demise of nearly everything else."

"This is a reference to our alleged shortcomings again, isn't it?" Bob asks wearily.

Cock answers the rhetorical question with an equally rhetorical silence.

Bob thinks about what Cock is saying. He is astounded. He's never heard of such a thing before. He does his best to wrap his brain around it.

"Okay," Bob says finally after a troubled silence. "But can you at least tell me *why* you do it?"

"It's not really a question of 'why,' Bob," Cock responds. "The mechanics of it are wired into us. You might as well ask why do you exhale carbon dioxide. It's a result of millions upon millions of years of successive organic technologies. These are simply the biomechanics of our species."

"But, what I mean," Bob clarifies, "is how do you stand it? How can you describe as holy the very condition which will lead to your demise? Why are you happy, or even content, with the certitude of soon being extinct?"

Cock patiently explains as best a miniature cockroach can to an uncomprehending human, "The more biodiversity on the planet, Bob, the more stable its web of life. And, ultimately, that's what matters most. For without a rich and complex, ever-evolving global web of life, nothing in itself could survive. The mosaic of life exists *in toto* —with no one part having any precedence over, or subservience to, any other. Life exists as one inextricable piece, and we live or die as a community, a community that extends to every piece of matter on the planet. Besides, Bob, don't you know that 99% of all species that have ever existed throughout time have become extinct? This was true millions of years before your time. Why shouldn't it be true millions of years afterwards? It is all part of the progressive process of building ever-more complex life systems."

Bob thinks the roach doth protest not enough.

"But don't you have *any* agony in knowing that someday not a trace of you—or your species, or your civilization—will ever exist?" Bob cries. "If you know all this, what reason could you possibly have for not going insane with pain?!"

Bob is so wrapped up in his own agony of being on the brink of extinction that he can't imagine how another being might be at peace with the thought.

"Well, Bob," Cock attempts to explain, "we all have our reasons. Each and every one of us performs our life functions with pride and peace of mind knowing that our lives and our biologies are perfectly geared for the good of the planet. This is a universally shared feeling of all things that exist in harmony with nature—with the knowledge of what is 'good' derived from being in perfect accord with the All That Is. It's sort of a bottomline, common ground of existence. But for me, personally, it's also something more and something less."

At this point, Cock moves certain body parts as to leave the impression with Bob that Bob is being taken into Cock's deepest confidence. Bob leans closer, unconsciously, trying to grasp the heart of it.

"For me, personally" Cock whispers, "it's also about the Karner blue butterfly."

"What?" says Bob.

"I want to contribute to a world where there will once again be Karner blue butterflies. Oh, maybe next time around they will be salmon-colored or lavender—maybe next time they will have opaque magenta wings instead of characteristic iridescent blue wings. Maybe next time they will feed on fields of pink hydrangeas instead of blue lupine. But what can I say—I'm a pushover for ethereal creatures. And it makes me happy knowing that I'm part of a process that is helping the planet to be in a position to create things again like butterflies."

Again, Bob is astounded.

"How did you ever hear about Karner blue butterflies?"

If the truth be known, Bob himself has never even heard of them. Only monarch butterflies. That's the only species that Bob can name off the top of his head. Of course, Bob is no lepidopterist, and certainly no Vladimir Nabokov, who *was* a lepidopterist and who named the Karner blue after a small village near the site where he first discovered the beauties—thousands of them—frolicking in a field under a glorious late-afternoon sun.

"We found a singular example enshrined in a block of glass," Cock answers. "There was a plaque inside floating beneath the specimen that read simply: *The Karner blue butterfly.*"

Bob understands instantly. A paperweight. From some kind of scientific supply store, he imagines. He's amazed at what the tombs of history will cough up for the unwitting pupils of the future. Bob remembers reading about scientists in his own time who had found a juvenile bear femur in the home-base hearth of a clan of Neanderthal hunters. The bone, found in the back of the cave near other artifacts such as stone tools, had a series of perfectly round holes drilled into it all in a perfectly straight line. The archeologists were beside themselves trying to decipher what the object could have meant to the bear-cave clan. Was it a musical instrument? Was it a primitive calendar? An accounting device? A child's toy? A game? A holy religious relic? Whatever its utility, this much was undeniable: it was an animal bone infused with human intent. And this by a group of near-humans that most thought of as little more than animals themselves. It was almost too much to consider. Modern humans were so comfortable thinking of the lowly Neanderthals as glorified ape-men. How utterly startling then—how shocking, how disruptive to modern self-aggrandizing prejudices—to discover that these creatures may have been more than slope-headed, upright wildebeests. That they may have had music, or leisure activities, or religion, or commerce. It was all too much to contemplate. It was all too much to place the trappings of humanity—the vestiges of modernity—onto these ice-age man-apes. The real fear, of course, was that some gorilla-loving biologist would walk into a camp of primates today and discover them eating peanuts from coconut bowls and playing cards. For if Neanderthals were so human-like in the midst of being so ape-like, it sends shivers up the slippery-slope of rigid spines to think about how human-like apes might actually be.

"You know, Cock," Bob says, rubbing his own slightly sloped forehead, "I think I've had enough for today. Can we cut out early and let me mull some of this over in private?"

"Of course, Bob," Cock consents. "I'll pick you up again tomorrow, as usual, after your treadmilling."

"Thank you," Bob says. "I won't forget this act of kindness."

Immediately afterwards, the two part ways and Bob heads off for an early retirement of rest and reflection.

Once alone in his sleep chamber, Bob is lost in a field of multiple musings. He goes to bed that night, restless and wrestling—thinking of ice-age Neanderthals blowing bone flutes with blue lips; wondering about the bouncing blue wavelengths of rainbow butterflies; pondering on the faintly bluish gas of ozone with its characteristic fresh, penetrating odor.

But at last, in the depths of a clear blue midnight, Bob falls asleep, utterly swaddled in melancholic thoughts of blue.

"So," Bob begins the next day in the dehydrated cocoa room, having considered the sum total of what he has learned at the hands of Cock (well, better said, at the six leg-arms and two antennae of Cock). Bob clears his throat for emphasis, and then adds, "Let's talk about why you actually brought me here, shall we?"

"I thought that's what we have been talking about," says Cock, confused. "Do you think I've gotten off topic?"

Bob shrugs his shoulders—he knows how sensitive Cock can be—while Cock continues, "We want you to be fully prepared when you finally walk into The Great Temple of the Arc. We want to make sure that you have as much information as possible in order to help us decipher the great mystery, the mystery of the Second Sun."

"Absolutely," Bob says. After all, if Bob is anything, he is a good sport. "It's just that I think we ought to move on to the heart of it."

"Well, exactly," Cock nods his antennae in agreement. "That is exactly where the mystery lies. At the heart of it, no doubt—like all good mysteries."

Cock begins pacing on the conference table. This is something that Cock hasn't done in a while and so Bob pays particular attention to what Cock is about to say.

"To begin," Cock says, "we have discovered a huge shrine— the biggest structure we've ever uncovered from your time period. And at the heart of it—in a large round room, what we call the Chamber of the Second Sun—are the religious artifacts that have made such an impression on our society and sent us into a philosophic titter."

Bob loves hearing the word "titter." It always makes him feel slightly naughty when it's used. In fact, hearing the word "titter" actually makes him behave in a tittering manner.

Ignoring Bob's idiosyncratic chortling, Cock continues, "It was in the heart of the Chamber of the Second Sun that we found the iconography that changed our worldview. Like Copernicus postulating a helio-centered solar system, our entire conception of the heavens was recast."

"Yes, yes, your worldview was shaken up. I get that. Just go on." Bob wants answers, not historic analogies. "What is it precisely that you found? Just what is it that I'm supposed to shed light on?"

Now Cock can't help but to stifle a little laugh, and to point out a species-wide characteristic habit of humans.

"It's fascinating, Bob—I'm an expert in this field, you know —but you humans can't seem to refrain from making puns, unconscious or not, no matter what it is you're talking about. Why, we've found references in every piece of written material that has survived. Reports of a guitar player who 'frets' about his music not being appreciated. Or that the 'focus' of the film was about so-and-so. A conference of seismologists in Los Angeles where an 'Earth-shaking' theory was revealed. Computer programmers who couldn't fix the Y2K problem, and so it was all for 'naught.' Ha ha! And now here you are—promising to 'shed light' on Sun worshipping. It really is a hoot —the way you humans write and speak. It's like you just never got over the joy of inventing language; and, subsequently, these playful, unconscious quirks utterly infused your communication patterns from the earliest times to the end. It is really something to behold."

Bob is not amused. At this point, he's not interested in gaining any more self-awareness, or species-awareness—he just wants to find out more about why the cockroaches think there was a Second Sun besides the one that currently exists and what may have led to its disappearance if it did exist.

Cock hears these thoughts of Bob—loud and clear—and so presses on in an officious and expeditious manner:

"In the innermost chamber in The Great Temple of the Arc, we found an amazing structure of iconography. It was a three-dimensional statue that plotted the arc of the Sun, twice. Or, more accurately, the parallel arcs of two Suns. This awe-inspiring, almost magical symbol was then found inscribed onto various religious artifacts —almost as a signature—throughout the inner chamber. We were amazed. Immediately, we were mesmerized by the simple, and yet profound, depiction of the Sun's arc through the sky as seen by an organism on the planet. We recognized it instantly as a timeless symbol, meaningful throughout all ages and for all beings. The path of the Sun in the sky—the arc—is one of the fundamental sacred geometrical shapes; and, like other fundamental patterns in our universe, such as the circle, the sphere, the spiral, and the double helix, it is a symbol not only of the movement of time, but of the essence of life itself. The circle, the sphere, and the double helix are all variations on the theme of eternity, whereas the spiral and the arc are symbols of time moving within eternity. Thus, the repetitive arc trajectory of the Sun's march across the sky of the spherical Earth simultaneously symbolizes both life and death, a beginning and ending, today and eternity. All of these profound concepts were crystallized into one amazing human artifact."

Here Cock pauses to catch his breath, and then continues:

"However, the artifact pointed to something even greater, something beyond sight, beyond the visible—a Second Sun, a second path in the sky, a second trajectory, a second sacred journey. What does that second journey symbolize? Is it metaphorical or literal? Figurative or functional? And if the Second Sun is literal, if there truly was a sibling to Sol, where has it gone? What has become of it? Why can we find no traces of it? The only clue we have at all is from the Mayans—they had a sacred calendar which ended, prophetically, on the Winter Solstice, December 21, 2012. That date eerily coincides with the disappearance of humans from the fossil record. Did the Mayans accurately predict the death of the Second Sun? And, if so, did the global-wide disasters have something to do with it? Finally, where did the Second Sun exist before it disappeared? It is these daunting mysteries, Bob, that you have been painstakingly transported to help unravel."

As Cock has been speaking, Bob's mind's eye has been alive with images: Apollo driving his fiery chariot across the sky from dawn to dusk; the horizon aglow with the big bald head of the Sun peaking over it and sinking below it; the scalding glare of the great sky-lamp at full salute in the midday stare like a heavenly Cyclops. Suddenly, Bob gets it. The Sun is everywhere at every time the king of life, the king of days—and all the while we, its loyal subjects, follow the majestic shadows it casts and honor its royal glow, a glow that heals us and hones us, searing us to a braised perfection.

Perhaps the Second Sun—or, as Bob now understands it, the repeated image of the one and only Sun's path—is merely an exuberant burst of expressive joy of the life that the Sun bestows upon us. Perhaps the majesty that is the life-giving powers of the Sun cannot be contained in one singular image of the Sun's path across Earth. Perhaps what seems a "second" Sun is merely the afterglow shadow of thankfulness infused upon the first and real Sun.

"No," Cock interrupts Bob's thoughts. "Of course, we thought

of that already. The Second Sun is not a mirror or reflection of the
first. That would be the Moon you're thinking of, and references to
the lunar cycle. Instead, the path of the Second Sun is a specific trajectory in its own right and this trajectory corresponds exactly with
the elliptical axis of the Earth's revolution around the current Sun.
Such a mathematically precise depiction can hardly be mere coinci-
dence. We believe it points to an actual Second Sun, a Sun which is
now nowhere present in the heavens."

Bob ingests this new information and attempts another avenue.
"Can I see an image of what you found?" he asks innocently.
"No!" Cock screams.
Bob nearly falls off his chair from the force of the negation.
"What is the matter?" Bob gasps, wiping chocolate off his
dashing Ghengis Kahn ensemble. He is very upset. This is one of his
favorite outfits.

"You must first see the structure in its natural context, Bob!
We don't want to show you any images beforehand because they may
prejudice you—or, worse yet, because they may steer you off in wrong
directions. For no image can duplicate the mesmerizing effect of the
icon itself, beheld in person and in context. We believe that the image
of the trajectories of the two Suns presents viewers with such a
powerfully religious experience that we do not want to jeopardize this
mission by exposing you to it prematurely. The iconography of the
trajectories of the two Suns must be approached in reverence and
awe—undoubtedly the attitude that the humans who made it expected
of pilgrims. Promise that you will approach this sacred object with
such deserved reverence!"

Bob doesn't know what to say—he hates to make promises
about things he knows nothing about—but it seems so important to
Cock, it seems so important to the success of the mission, that against
his first impulse and possibly his better judgment, Bob promises…sort
of.

"I promise to approach the shrine and the objects nestled inside it with all the appropriate reverence they deserve."

Cock understands that Bob's statement is a bit of a hedge, but right now Bob is all the roaches have to being able to solve the mystery. Cock accepts the promise as best Cock can.

"All right," Cock says slowly, "but also please promise me that tonight—the last night before we leave on our trek to the Temple—you will meditate on these things and you will prepare in all ways possible to open your soul to this experience."

Bob answers with complete sincerity and earnestness, "I promise to prepare my soul as if it were for the bitter end. I promise to do all in my power to help you understand the significance of what you have found."

This statement, finally, proves satisfactory for Cock, and Cock tells Bob so. Cock then suggests they call it a day and prepare—in body, mind, and spirit—for the great journey ahead.

"Good enough," says the tired human.

"Sweet dreams, Bob," Cock says with both affection and trepidation as Bob pushes back his chair from the table.

And then, as Cock watches, Bob—the roach's sole link to historical and spiritual enlightenment—plods out of the room, adjusting his Mongolian embroidered jacket and tugging at the crack of his Mongolian cut pantaloons.

Before he leaves for a final well-earned evening of rest, Bob takes a last look around the training facility. He cannot shake off the feeling: It is a military compound. It is a war room. And the war that is raging the most excruciatingly is the war inside his own bag of bones, springing forth as it does from his struggle against himself and against what used to be his own historical moment.

That night's sleep is heavy and full of star-spangled dreams for Bob—embroiled in a starry, starry night—where he conjures anxious visions of heat and flames and explosions. Bob soars through hoops of fire. He flies through burning cauldrons of stars. A tingling starts at the base of his spine and shoots up through his trunk. The fire in his belly boils over until he explodes into great balls of fire himself, brandished throughout the heavens. From another vantage point, Bob looks at himself twinkling in the night sky. For a brief moment, it is a peaceful sky, enjoyed from a peaceful planet. But, then, a great cacophony envelops the cosmos, a cataclysmic fusillade that lights up every corner of the universe. And, then—as he gasps, gazing at the aftermath—Bob finds the heavens are littered with suns and their explosions, the sons of suns.

He stands paralyzed, peering in fearful wonder at the solitary night sky, a sky that now glistens madly with stars and the remnants of stars.

Unexpected Memory Interruption #5:
Is There a Soldier in the House?

Bob's father is a peacetime soldier. It must be yet another indignity for a man so infused with peacetime rage. For Bob's father is embroiled in the psychic wars he has fought — back there on a little dirt farm in the bowels of Indiana — and he is ever eager to prove himself a man, having already been subjugated to so many unmanly events on his way to manhood.

Bob's father rants, Bob's father raves. Bob's father coos. In between fits, Bob's father proclaims the sweetest of fatherly love for his entire brood, but especially for the other little man in the house: Bob.

But poor little man Bob. So unable to read the body language of a peacetime soldier. Never knowing if his childish antics or adolescent curiosities will be met with the open palms of father's love or the closed fists of father's rage. Bob can't read his father. Though he tries like the most diligent Talmudic scholar — every nuance analyzed, every movement memorized, every behavior studied and stoically stored in the stockpile of memories of father's emotions, so that later, when similar conditions in the household arise, Bob can, like a computer, compare every previous action and response to predict a likely outcome of the current situation.

Except it never works.

No two events, no two situations, ever produce similar outcomes. The illogic of it all drives Bob to tears and terror. He is such a good student, such a good little soldier, and he studies his father so assiduously — but why doesn't Bob ever come any closer to being able to stay out of the way of those paternal, one-two punches?

This is the puzzle of the peacetime soldier.

And if the puzzle of the peacetime soldier isn't a puzzle that Bob can figure out, then he will surround himself with puzzles that he can.

If Bob can't figure out why his father would rather oil and polish his guns than take Bob out to a ballgame; if Bob can't figure out why his father relentlessly hammers his mother and sister, driving them to tears and worse; if Bob can't figure out why his father places a gun to his own head rather than face his life and all its mistakes straight on—if Bob can't figure out these things, then he will indeed surround himself with safer puzzles, with numbers, with codes, with logical problems harboring logical solutions, with anything but the unpredictable humans who have shadowed his world.

This is the puzzle of the peacetime soldier.

And this is the puzzle's answer to the peacetime soldier's son.

Chapter 5:

Bob Unravels the Secret Mystery of the Alien Future Civilization and In So Doing, His Mind Understands Where He Has Come From (but His Heart Implodes)

Bob is in his Earth suit and Cock is propitiously placed in the perch. The two linger outside the elevator on the edge of the ashen jungle. It is eerily quiet, with no roach movement to be seen. Bob is expecting a vehicle for their journey to arrive. He sees none. Instead, they stand, unmoving.

"What are we waiting for?" Bob asks. Now that the fateful day has arrived, he is eager for the expedition to begin.

"The pilot," Cock answers, without elaborating. In fact, Bob notices that Cock is curiously quiet this morning.

But at least the information puts Bob at ease. He understands the concept of pilots and airplanes and flight. In fact, by coming to the future with Cock, Bob forfeited several thousand frequent flyer miles, just as he was about due for a free flight to Ireland. Bob daydreams about the once luscious green isle and regrets not having learned more about the Celts before it all ended. It was on his list of things to do. Unfortunately, he just never got around to it.

In the meantime, daydreams aside, several more minutes go by and still nothing happens.

At last, anxious to get going, Bob breaks the silence.

"Really, Cock, what are we waiting for?"

"I told you, Bob," comes the curt answer, "we're waiting for our pilot."

Bob sees, clearly, that there is no conversation to be had down this avenue, so he cans it for the moment and tries to focus on the journey ahead and all that he has learned about the science of life.

While Bob is deep in contemplation, from the eastern branch of the path a cloud of ashen dust appears. By the voluminous billows, Bob concludes it must be a tank of some sort that approaches; but, as the cloud closes in, he sees that the dust storm is caused not by the cockroach equivalent of a panzer tank, but simply by a huge roach catapulted along by buzzing wings.

The roach is the biggest specimen Bob has yet seen. It's a giant among roaches, big and strong. And it scurries up to them with a speed that belies its stature.

Cock performs the formal introductions.

"Deborah—Bob. Bob—Deborah."

Bob is speechless. However, Deborah is not.

"Glad to meet you, Bob. I've heard so much about you," Deborah says with squeaky new vocal cords.

"Hey, you can talk!" shouts Bob.

"Yes, that's why I'm late," Deborah squeaks. "I needed a few adjustments—it seems I was emanating wavelengths beyond human audio perception."

"Hey, you can talk!" Bob shouts again.

"Yes, Bob," Deborah laughs. "We've already established that fact."

Deborah turns to Cock and thinks: He's so much shorter in person!

Cock thinks back: It's not polite to think about him in front of him.

Then Cock turns to Bob and explains, "The trip is likely to be highly stressful for you, Bob—traveling great distances, seeing the recovering wasteland that is now the Earth, confronting the tattered remains of your dead civilization, and so forth—so we concluded that your being able to communicate directly with another being would be psychologically beneficial. Also, it alleviates me from translation duties so that I may concentrate on scientific and other observations."

Hearing Cock's little speech, Bob is now forced to think about the tattered remains of his dead civilization. Up until now, he had been doing a pretty good job of steadfastly ignoring that fact. Darn that penetrating Cock!—Cock is always reminding Bob of something he'd rather not think about.

"Are you ready?" Cock interrupts Bob's thinking.

"I guess," Bob says, less sure than he was a few minutes ago. Then he takes stock of the vehicular situation. "Okay, so the pilot's here, but where's the plane?"

"The pilot *is* the plane," says Cock. "In our language it's the same word. Just like in one of your languages, 'to consume' and 'to govern' were the same words."

Having never vacationed in Cambodia, Bob isn't quite sure what Cock is talking about, but it doesn't much matter because he is not paying attention anyway.

Instead, Bob is staring, somewhat impolitely by roach etiquette, at Deborah. Deborah, in turn, rears up on strong hind legs and stretches out four powerful upper leg-arms, in what Deborah intends to be a friendly gesture.

"Welcome to the friendly skies of Deborah," Deborah offers jovially.

It's the last thing Bob hears before he hits the ground in a faint.

After a quick emergency trip to the hospitality house—where Bob is plied with the wonders of more cocoa IV infusions, and subsequently equipped with a large portable tank of the stuff—the trio ascends to the surface of the Earth refreshed and ready for flight.

Not that he ever would have expected it, or wished it, but Bob now finds himself strapped to the belly of a flying roach, with Cock safely zipped up in a transparent balcony as his reticent flight companion. As Bob settles in to his predicament, Deborah's powerful sets of wings—both sets, the shorter, thick forewings, and the longer, graceful hind wings—begin flapping at many thousand times per minute, carrying Deborah and her cargo up above the top of the fern forest and toward the great land to the south.

It's amazing, thinks Bob, as he feels himself lifted effortlessly into the air.

"No big deal," notes Cock. "We can lift 20 times our body weight."

This odd symbiotic package flies in graceful arcs of spectacular aerial undulations, with Deborah's powerful wings beating in a fury, bringing them to the zenith in their trajectory and then resting in the glide downward toward the nadir, at which point the great wings drum again. Their path in the sky, if plotted on a two-dimensional graph, would mirror exactly a sine-cosine wave. Mathematical consistency and accuracy—all contained within the beating of a roach's wings.

As their altitude climbs higher and higher, Bob discovers a newfound fear of heights and closes his eyes tight. But he doesn't want to miss the panorama. So, when Bob finds he has the nerve, he periodically opens his eyes and peers down at the Earth below. The group is more than high enough to get a bird's-eye view—which hardly seems proper to Bob, seeing how there are no birds in the present configuration of life-forms—and from this vantage, he can make out certain features on the landscape like the meditation huts and the lone sacred dais here and there. However, these roach structures punctuate the landscape with less frequency the farther they travel south, and after a while it is only the sickly palm and fern leaves that cover a land interrupted by vast stretches of rusted rocks and churning volcanoes.

They keep a steady path, flying south by southwest, and when Bob feels sick to his stomach from vertigo, he takes another swig of his cocoa and wraps his hands, in a frenzy, tighter around the hemp-rope halter that holds him in place. You know, he thinks to himself while contemplating the scorched Earth below, the trouble with you,

Bob, is that you never traveled enough before it all went to the birds
—so now look at the kind of misbegotten world you get to see.

Bob floats in and out of cocoa-induced states of awareness—
eventually letting go of his initial fear of roach flying—while the scenes
passing below him constitute an alien landscape of dunes and parched
lands, jungle rot and saltless seas. At one point, Bob thinks he sees
something that resembles the huge, dry basin of what once could
have been the Great Lakes. It sends a shiver down his spine to think
so, and he clings tighter to the gear that holds him in place.

They fly like this for three days and three nights, resting each
evening at tiny expedition camps along the way, until at last they are
but a short day's hike from their destination.

On this third evening, the group rests and meditates in the
hospitality house that has been prepared in advance for Bob's arrival.
They are gathered in fellowship, lingering over their cocoa dregs, with
the various scientists and archeologists who staff the camp. It is Bob
who begins the after-cocoa talk, interrupting the thinking that is
already taking place at breakneck speed.

"You know," Bob says, breaking what he thinks is silence, "I
never asked you how you came across The Great Temple of the Arc in
the first place. If it is so isolated from your main hubs of activity,
sequestered here in this distant land, how did you ever discover it?"

"We followed the finger of the sky," Cock answers.

Bob is not sure what to make of this.

"Yes, Bob, all questions come from the sky and are answered
there, too," adds Deborah.

Bob still is not sure what to make of this.

"A meteorite," Cock explains.

Ah, Bob nods his head in recognition.

"A great blue-green fireball crashed into the Earth and when
we went to explore it, we discovered the Temple. The meteor had
landed right smack in the middle of it."

At this point, in an attempt to help Bob understand completely, their host and noted archeologist Gregor Hermes stands up and embarks upon his favorite party trick. As the other guests appreciably wave their respective antennae (save for Bob, of course), Gregor rises on hind legs and adjusts the antennae above its head into two great arcs coming to meet each other, producing an ellipse-shaped oval. Then, with much concentration and the rising and falling of spiracles, Gregor slips into a trance-like state. Shortly afterwards, small shoots of electricity spark in between the antennae, like tiny lightning branches shooting back and forth, finally composing a thin electric film. Upon this thin bluish layer a ghostly image appears of a blue-green meteor flying through the sky and crashing into the ashen Earth. Then, suddenly, the images vanish and Gregor falls over exhausted.

"Wow," Bob says without thinking, "can Gregor get cable, too?"

Deborah helps Gregor—who is spent for the rest of the evening —into Gregor's sleeping slot and then continues explaining in a more conventional manner to Bob, "It's a little something Gregor invented to entertain guests. We're hoping to find some additional use for it."

"No doubt," mumbles Bob, thinking of things the roaches will never understand, like Nielsen ratings, sweeps, prime-time, and canned laughter.

And then Cock, ever to the point, addresses the original question again.

"After the meteorite crashed, we had reports of a massive crater. Except that it wasn't in the shape of a crater. Initial fly-overs indicated that the shape was not circular, but rectangular, and thus couldn't have been caused by the meteorite. But, regardless, there clearly was a huge opening in the ground. At first we thought, odd as it might be, the meteor had created the impression. But as more reports came in, and as we sent more scientists to the site, it became clear that the meteor had merely shattered a thin shield of sulfuric ice that had been covering a huge structure beneath it. At last we understood: We were not seeing the huge, impact-crater of a small meteorite, at all, but we were seeing the inside of a huge, buried structure that a small meteorite had crashed into. It turned out to be the largest structure we have ever discovered from your time—what we later dubbed The Great Temple of the Arc. And there in the dead center of it, a few meters from the remains of the meteorite, lay the undeniable proof that yours was a Sun-worshipping culture: the Inner Chamber of the Two Suns."

At this point, Cock turns quite emotional, veritably quaking with feeling.

"And now, at long last, our mission is almost over. Tomorrow, at last—with Bob's selfless assistance—we will discover the meaning of the Second Sun."

The roaches raise their cocoa bowls in unison and Bob slowly lifts his to join them, all the while registering an uncanny queasy feeling in his stomach. He feels like he used to in college, after he'd eaten too many french fries.

And, then, it's lights out at camp Gregor, as everyone prepares for the ensuing momentous day.

The next morning, the group is up early. Good-byes are exchanged all around and Bob goes so far as to shake a leg with Gregor. (After all, Bob is safely ensconced in his protective Earth suit, and thus isn't really touching Gregor.) Deeply honored, Gregor conjures up a disembodied vision of smiling human teeth between his antennae and, although Bob knows Gregor means it as a visual good-bye gift, Bob can't help thinking about it as a tacky toothpaste commercial. Undoubtedly, Gregor would have been offended by Bob's interpretation, but for the moment Gregor knows nothing, passed out as Gregor is from the exertion of these creative labors.

Formal farewells accomplished, Deborah, Cock, and Bob set out—on foot and on roach leg—to The Great Temple of the Arc. The terrain is particularly treacherous, with sulfuric gases belching up from open sores in the Earth, not to mention weakened topsoil that caves in upon the slightest pressure. Cock tells Bob the current scientific theory is that there was once a thriving civilization living under this very ground and that the pockets in the soil are likely buried structures which crumble with the slightest disturbance. Because of their holy mission and sacred preoccupations, the roaches haven't had the resources or the inclination to explore the entire area to find out what is actually down there. Instead, they tread gingerly to the Temple, the area that has already been serendipitously opened up for them, like a gift from the heavens.

After half a day's hike, the trio comes to rest in front of a huge cave-like opening in front of a small mountain.

"This is it," says Cock.

Bob looks around, unimpressed.

"From the way you described it," Bob says, "I expected a huge open-air amphitheater—not an underground cavern into a mountain."

"It opens up from the inside," Cock responds. "And the easiest way to get inside is through this opening tunnel. After we travel about a quarter mile, suddenly there is no top. The cave leads into a huge structure that's had its roof torn off—that's the area where the meteorite is."

They start to enter the dark entrance, but Deborah stops them to clarify something, "By the way, Bob—just so you understand—the mountain *is* the temple. The structure has simply been reclaimed by the Earth. We enter by this tunnel because it's quicker to go through it than over it."

Jesus, Bob thinks, looking at the mountain again. He doesn't think he's ever seen a structure this large. But he is wrong. He has seen a structure this large before. In fact, he has seen *this* structure before. He's even been inside it before. He simply doesn't recognize it in its present, half-buried, multimillion-year-old condition.

They enter the cave—which is dimly illuminated by

phosphorescent rocks—and walk in silence for about a quarter of a mile. Then, just as Cock attested, the area opens up and shortly afterward the sky floats above a massive hole in the ground, a mammoth building without a roof standing half-buried in the Earth.

Caught off guard by the sudden change in light, Bob trips on something and skids face-first to the ground.

"Are you okay?" Cock inquires from inside the perch.

"Yes," Bob says. But as he begins to pick himself up, his gloved hand brushes against something sticking out of the ground. Bob begins to tug at it, and soon a piece comes off in his hand. He examines it carefully.

"What do you have there, Bob?" Cock asks.

As far as Bob can tell, it looks like copper wire encased in protective tubing. He's not sure what to say about it.

Cock looks at it.

"Oh, that stuff. There's miles of it in here. It's like a nervous system for the structure. It probably conveyed the Sun's impulses to other centers."

Bob thinks it looks like telephone or electrical wiring, but he doesn't offer any opinion. Instead, Bob kneels down to where he got the piece and begins to dust off the area around it. What he finds are some broken tiles. He rubs a little harder—marble.

Bob is kneeling on marble tiles.

Then it hits him. The thought of it overwhelms him—that some human cut and carefully placed the very tiles he is kneeling on many millions of years ago is enough to make his heart break. It suddenly hits him with full emotional impact that he is standing in the bowels of some building where other humans once freely strode.

Cock senses the emotional shift in Bob—in fact, the raging emotions interfere with Cock's ability to read Bob's thoughts. Worried that they are running out of time, Cock signals Deborah to take them quickly to the center of the structure where the meteorite and Chamber of the Second Sun await.

Without any protest from Bob—which the roaches take, correctly, as a bad sign—Deborah picks up Bob and Cock and flies them down a huge hallway. On either side of the hallway are openings to other parts of the structure—but they don't stop to explore any of these passageways. Instead, Deborah plops the passengers down at the end of the hallway, in the center of a huge, open area.

"Over there," Deborah says and points Bob in the direction of a silver carcass sticking out of a crumbling half-wall. "The meteorite."

Before he moves in closer to the object, Bob lifts his right hand to his chest, where Cock is stationed in the perch.

"Get out," Bob says.

"But why?" asks Cock, not moving.

"I want some privacy," is all that Bob answers.

Cock hears the determination in Bob's voice and decides not to object. Cock crawls onto Bob's hand and Bob hands over the tiny cargo to Deborah. Cock promptly self-attaches to Deborah's abdomen, being careful not to fall into a breathing spiracle.

Only after transferring Cock, does Bob then slowly walk over to the object—the so-called meteorite—and examine it.

It is not a chunk of rock. It is a chunk of metal—a satellite. By the color and reflectivity of it, Bob guesses it's made of titanium, virtually indestructible. The satellite even has a broken antennae hanging off of it. Bob approaches the man-made object and reverently touches it. When his hand makes contact, tears come to his eyes. He walks slowly around the object and on the far side finds an identification plate. The letters "NASA" stand out to him, of course, but there is more writing that is partially obscured by dust and dirt. He rubs it off with vigorous strokes and reads the name underneath: "Cassini-I."

Bob recognizes it instantly: It is NASA's top-secret Cassini-I space probe. Bob knows about it from the DOD top security work he did while at SIMS, Inc. The Cassini-I satellite was a prototype of solar system explorers built in the 1970s, the largest plutonium-powered object ever built in its time. Its secret mission was to travel to the outer limits of the solar system where a massive dense, dark object had been detected. Cassini-I was to get data on the object so that scientists could analyze what the mysterious phenomenon with an erratic orbit might be. However, the craft had never been heard from once past Jupiter and the DOD files Bob had seen deemed the craft destroyed or lost in space.

Apparently, the craft was not destroyed, merely lost and eventually homesick, and whether by freak of nature or design of planetary gravitational forces had found its way back again—a few million years later—bringing along its deadly power-pack payload.

The plutonium poison that Cassini-I was carrying immediately makes Bob think of its successor, the even more poisonous space probe named, simply, Cassini.

The top secret Cassini-I was the forerunner of the publicly announced Cassini space probe which was launched to much fanfare in 1998 and propelled by a twice-as-deadly plutonium load on its journey through the solar system to acquire knowledge about Earth's extraterrestrial neighbors. Bob remembers that this second Cassini satellite was scheduled to swing past the Earth in the fall of 1999 to get a boost from the gravitational field of the planet. Bob wonders if it, too, carried the curse of its namesake and got caught in the gravitational pull of the Earth and likewise came crashing down?

If so, Bob realizes in a flash that Cassini, with a payload of enough plutonium to kill every human and animal on the planet thousands of times over, could itself have made the Y2K bug completely mute. With every living thing on the planet made instantly dead from plutonium poisoning, any bombs and nuclear reactors that subsequently collapsed would have fallen on deaf (that is, dead) ears. Preparing obsessively for one catastrophe, the planet quite possibly ignored another. And even if it wasn't Cassini that fell to Earth that fall, it could have just as easily been any one of a number of poison-powered satellites or rockets that the government routinely sent up without ever telling the pubic about it. Either way, the prototype of these agents of catastrophe was resting here silently, buried, in this underground tomb, a testament to the awesome power that humans had tried, unsuccessfully, to harness.

In the end, Bob wonders, does it matter what killed the humans: a Cassini-like plutonium catastrophe or a Y2K-like induced nuclear catastrophe? No, Bob realizes, of course it doesn't matter. The end result to humanity and the destructive effect on the Earth would be the same. Because even if all the humans were simultaneously wiped out by something else entirely—say, an infectious virus, or a gigantic asteroid—the Earth itself would still be in grave danger from the poisonous arsenal that human civilization had accumulated prior to its extinction. With no humans left to oversee them, to dismantle them, to disarm them, the bombs would have still exploded and the nuclear reactors would have still melted down, all on their own unattended accord. With no humans to watch over them, the chemical poisons, the radioactive materials, the man-made storehouses of anthrax and PCBs would eventually have escaped their containers and gone about their baneful business of polluting the Earth—to a disastrous and perhaps irrecoverable degree.

From the roaches' perspective, seeing only the evidence of cataclysmic destruction in the archeological record, they would have no idea what *actually* caused the global meltdown; they would never know if the humans were even in existence when the corrupt house of cards that humans built took its final, destructive bow.

With an anguish veering toward madness, Bob realizes how pointless it all really was. How completely humans had gutted the Earth. How once the evil genie—the evil genie of splitting the atom—was out of the bottle, how utterly impossible it was to put him safely back inside.

Bob looks around at his present environment, the demolished artifact to what he has been thinking.

This place, this cavern of horrors, just what was it, Bob wondered?

In answer to his own question, Bob scrutinizes the space more closely. He sees past the melding of dirt and structure. He sees past the mold and gray vines to the concrete and marble beneath. He sees past the present and directly back into the past.

Stores with no doors all facing a wide hallway. A huge open court. Four million square feet of connected space. Miles of telephone and electrical wires. Suddenly Bob knows this place. He knows it inside out the way he knows his worst dreams.

He is in the belly of the beast. Bob is in the remains of the biggest mall the United States had ever seen: The Mall of America, just outside of what was once Minneapolis, Minnesota, his adopted hometown.

Was this it? Was this palace of consumption—now solemnly serving as the tomb of Cassini-I—was this The Great Temple of the Arc, the holy chamber of Sun worshipping?

As the tears stream down Bob's face, he can only conclude that the Second Sun the roaches are concerned with was the family of Cassini probes—the fireballs from the sky, the arcs of radiation with which mankind polluted its skies and its soul. Was this the high truth of his world that Bob must now tell Cock and Deborah? Is this what all the fuss has been about? That some mutant son of the H-bomb, a plutonium-powered satellite, was the Second Sun humans worshipped? That man-made radiation was the Second Sun to which humans gave their ultimate allegiance?

Bob instantly comprehends the utter stupidity of creating nuclear weapons and energy, with their deadly radioactive waste and their timebomb aftermath consequences. The Y2K computer bug was absolutely nothing compared to this. The grand and deadly folly was this: Humans had tried to harness the energy that fueled the Sun. But once Pandora's box had been opened, there was no hope for anything, even the Earth itself.

How could Bob now face these innocent roach creatures and tell them the truth about men's souls?

While Bob weeps, Cock and Deborah are in constant antennae communication trying to decipher what disturbing things are racing through Bob's nervous system.

Can you get a read on him?! a frightened Cock signals.

No, Deborah responds, there's too much emotional interference to understand what he's thinking.

Finally, some tiny piece of it gets through and Cock realizes that Bob thinks the meteorite is the sacred object in the Chamber of the Second Sun. Cock realizes Bob has made a grave mistake.

No wonder Bob is upset, Cock signals Deborah, he thinks we've shown him the meteorite as the sacred object in the Chamber of the Second Sun.

Of course! Deborah responds enthusiastically. He thinks we don't understand his religion.

To set the matter straight, Deborah approaches Bob and says to him gently, "No, Bob, you don't understand. This isn't the Chamber of the Second Sun. The chamber, and its sacred object, is over there."

And with that, Deborah breaks Bob's no-touch policy for a second time that day, placing two leg-arms on Bob's shoulders and turning him around to face the Chamber of the Second Sun.

Because of the Earth suit he is wearing, Bob can't simply wipe away his tears, so he stares for a few seconds in the direction that Deborah has pointed him in and waits for his vision to clear.

When it does, Bob receives the final blow to his system.

There, standing as if it had been bolted into place yesterday, are two perfectly drawn half-ellipses, side by side, of the Sun's arc as it rises from the low belly of one horizon, travels to the tip of its arc at the midday point, and then sinks back down to the belly of the opposite horizon.

Standing before him is a plastic representation of the yellow arc that the Sun makes every day in the sky above the Earth. It is a resin representation of a colossal event. An event observed by every form of life since life began, since the first bacteria rose from the carbon cycle to salute the day and to begin a chain of events that continues even now.

For this is the story of life on Earth: every day for billions of years the Sun appears on one edge of the eastern horizon, makes a great arc to the top of the sky and then completes a mirror journey back down to the edge of the other horizon. And this simple pattern, repeated endlessly over countless spans of time, eventually produced life on the very globe where such arcs repeatedly came to pass. Surely, every speck of life recognizes, understands, and respects this arc. Surely, every speck of life, every life-form knows—somewhere on some level, on some deep cellular level—that without this arc there would be no life. Surely, every speck of life on the planet is programmed to understand the life-giving power of the yellow arc of the Sun's trajectory over the Earth.

And here it is now—at least an uncanny representation of it —standing in front of him. Multiplied times two. Bob is viewing the arcs, the double arc, the two yellow arcs placed side by side, and seeing them for the millionth time and first time, all at once.

Here at last is the mystery of the Second Sun. The plastic double arches—in the food court. And how could Bob, the bridge between worlds, ever bring himself to tell his virtuous hosts what this symbol actually stood for? How could he explain how the decadent human desire for fried foods and convenience could ever be confused with something so sacred as worship and reverence of the Sun?

He walks closer to the yellow object and sees something harrowing embedded in it. There, hermetically sealed in little plastic slots, are instamatic photographs of children having birthday parties. Instinctually, Bob is drawn to one particular photograph—with horror, he recognizes an image of his younger self, holding his four-year-old niece at a birthday party at this very same food court restaurant. There is Bob from Minnesota, holding a smiling Lauren, and waving at his sister behind the camera. With a flash of sickening insight, Bob realizes that this snapshot of everyday family life is his only legacy left to the future—the sole remaining evidence of his life, a moment that bespeaks nothing of his life's work and his expertise around computers and Y2K—and that this is the singular random clue from which the roaches tracked him down.

With his heart breaking into pieces all around him and with the harsh reality of his world crashing in on him, Bob turns his back on the yellow, double arcs and faces Deborah and Cock.

He waves at them. Confused, they wave back.

And then Bob rips off his Earth suit.

Cock and Deborah scream "NO!"—but it is too late.

Bob fries in an instant.

Even before his suit hits the ground, Bob is gone, zapped into a column of dust that slowly crumbles and floats to the fetid soil, resting—curiously—beside a series of ash piles.

Cock and Deborah rush over to the place where Bob had been. But Bob Bridges is nothing but a pile of ashes situated among other similar piles of ashes.

With heavy hearts, Cock and Deborah turn to each other.

Damn, cries Cock. Why do they keep doing that?!

I don't know, shrugs Deborah, but I think we should make the suit inescapable next time.

Yeah, Cock nods. Something they can't get out of themselves.

Dejection spreads all around them. Then Cock signals, Did you get *any* of his thoughts before he went?

No, Deborah responds wearily, just a few images of the Sun rising and setting in the sky, and then a disjointed flash of a chocolate milkshake.

Damn! thinks Cock again. I really thought we had the right one this time. I really thought we did. Wait until Pliny hears about this!

Don't worry about Pliny, Deborah signals softly. You can just never tell with humans. You should know that by now. You take care of them. You rescue them from certain annihilation. You try to teach them something. But, ultimately, they just keep showing up for the food.

But I really thought it would be different with him, Cock answers. Cock simply cannot fathom it: You know, Bob seemed special somehow. Smarter than the rest. And I really kind of liked the guy— you know, for a human.

No use crying over spilled carbon, Deborah shrugs. We simply need to figure out what to do differently next time.

Next time? What next time? Cock signals. The window of the time differential is almost up, and besides, no one else who is qualified will volunteer for spacetime travel.

No one except me, you mean, Deborah responds.

Deborah, I thought we agreed that it was enough to risk my life, not yours, too.

Cock cannot believe what he is receiving. Does Cock dare to hope again?

You made it back safely, Deborah answers. Why shouldn't I? Besides, a lot of good it does our future progeny for us to be completely different sizes.

Cock's heart is uplifted.

I thought you said that was all over long ago, Cock ventures.

And to this plaintiff cry of the heart, Deborah responds, No, it never was. Now I've got a job to do, too, Cock. Where you've been, I can follow. What you've had to do, I can be a part of, also. I'm no good at being noble, Cock, but I can undergo shrinkage and go back to Bob's world and bring back another human, and then maybe we'll discover the answer to the Second Sun, or maybe we'll be lost in the final moments yet again. But either way, we'll be the same size again, and that ought to mean something.

Yes, it does, Cock proclaims. It means everything to me!

Then it's decided, Deborah signals. Let's not debate it any further.

Cock's antennae nod fiercely in agreement.

As they stare down at the pile that once was Bob, Cock signals, Any idea who's next on the list?

Yes, I memorized the name, Deborah responds. It's another alliterative specimen named 'Penny Perkins.'

Let's just hope this Penny proves a steadier candidate than Bob, Cock notes.

Indeed, Deborah agrees.

And with a respectful nod to the pile that used to be Bob, Cock says out loud, using his vocal cords, as a kind of eulogy and last rites for this favorite human, "Rest in peaceful pieces, Bob Bridges. Rest in peaceful peace."

And with that, the paramours head back to the tunnel, making their way out of The Great Temple of the Arc, Cock clinging happily to Deborah's warm underbelly.

But as Cock and Deborah leave, what they don't see, or what they fail to notice, is the ever-so-slight movement of the pile of ashes. It could be the wind. It could be the sulfur rumbling beneath the Earth. It could be the breath of God.

Whatever it is, it is also this: the birth of some new life-form —some tiny, microscopic, new organism whose descendants will one day reinvent oxygenic respiration and again light the path for life on Earth to bloom once more with full force.

Unexpected Memory Interruption #6:
When I Was

In the instant before Bob is vaporized, a knowing image comes back to haunt him. He remembers now. For a tiny fraction of an instant, he remembers.

Bob is a bug. A bug at the bottom of the ocean. Bob is a bug at the bottom of the ocean hemmed in on all sides by the enormous pressures of water and consciousness.

At last—at long, lingering last—Bob understands his predicament, a predicament he now realizes that he shares with all beings everywhere separated from nature, separated from the All That Is.

And now, in this tiny fraction of an instant—the sharpest, smallest edge of what we call the present—just before the lights go out, just before his parts are disassembled, reassembled, reconstituted, and made ready for their next manifestation, just then Bob hears the final parting words that he will hear in this life, words that drift into his quickly vaporizing mind, words that seep into his evaporating consciousness from the vast outer reaches of spacetime:

"But, Bob, it is not *we* who are the bugs."

With his last dying embers of consciousness, Bob recognizes the imprint of Cock. It is Cock, it seems, who will have the last word.

But—*NO!*—before it can be over, Bob reemerges briefly from the void, and states the truth for himself.

"It is not *they* who are the bugs," responds Bob. "It is not they who are the bugs."

At long last, Bob understands.

And then, Bob, as a Bob, is no longer.

Meet Bob Bug.

Afterword

While this story is a work of fiction, much of the technical data and scientific conjectures are based on real-life facts and our current understanding of the makeup of reality.

While writing this work, I was very much indebted to the resources I used in research, and I urge interested readers to review these fascinating materials firsthand—and quickly, too, while there is still time:

Books

Time Bomb 2000: What the Year 2000 Computer Crisis Means to You!, by Edward Yourdon & Jennifer Yourdon (Prentice Hall PTR: Upper Saddle River, NJ, 1997, revised 1999)

Y2K: An Action Plan, by Victor Porlier (HarperCollins, 1999)

The Year 2000 Software Problem: Quantifying the Costs and Assessing the Consequences, by Capers Jones (Addison-Wesley, 1997)

Apocalypse 2000: The Book of Revelation, edited by John Miller (Seastone, an imprint of Ulysses Press: Berkeley, CA, 1998)

The Philosophical Programmer: Reflections on the Moth in the Machine, by Daniel Kohanski (St. Martin's Press: New York, 1998)

The Compleat Cockroach: A Comprehensive Guide to the Most Despised (and Least Understood) Creature on Earth, by David George Gordon (Ten Speed Press, Berkeley, CA, 1996)

The Ages of Gaia: A Biography of Our Living Earth, by James Lovelock (1998)

Gaia: A New Look at Life on Earth, by James Lovelock (Oxford University Press, 1987)

Microcosmos: Four Billion Years of Evolution from our Microbial Ancestors, by Lynn Margulis, Dorion Sagan, and Lewis Thomas (University of California Press, 1997)

Symbiotic Planet: A New Look at Evolution, by Lynn Margulis (Basic Books, 1998)

The Web of Life: A New Scientific Understanding of Living Systems, by Fridj Caprof (Anchor Books, Doubleday, 1996)

Articles

"An Essay on the Principle of Population As It Affects the Future Improvement of Society," by Robert Malthus, c. 1790.

"Will Humans Overwhelm the Earth? The Debate Continues," by Malcolm W. Browne in *The New York Times*, 12/08/1998, F5 at col. 1.

"Once He Devised Germ Weapons: Now He Defends Against Them," by William J. Broad and Judith Miller in *The New York Times*, 11/03/1998, F1 at col. 2.

"Germ Weapons: Only in the Soviet Union's Past or in the New Russia's Future?" by Judith Miller and William J. Broad in *The New York Times*, 12/28/1998, A1 at col. 1 and continued on A11 at col. 1.

"12.31.99: The Y2K Nightmare" by Robert Sam Anson in *Vanity Fair*, no. 461 (January 1999), pages 80-84, 139-144.

On-line Articles

Utne Reader's *Y2K Citizen's Action Guide*:
http://www.utne.com/y2k

Gary North's *Reality Check* newsletter and Web site:
http://www.garynorth.com

Web Sites

Y2K Today
http://www.y2ktoday.com

Westergaard Y2K
http://www.y2ktimebomb.com

The Year 2000 Information Center
http://www.year2000.com

The Cassandra Project
http://www.cassandraprojct.org

Y2K Links from Alternative Media
http://www.altmedia.miningco.com/msub26.htm

Acknowledgements

When publishing a first book there are untold numbers of people to acknowledge and thank. I can only begin to thank a small portion of them here, so in advance let me apologize for what is sure to be many omissions.

That said, let me begin by thanking readers of the book in manuscript form: Debra Raftery, Janice Perkins, Paula Martinac, Jill Dearman, Rob Maskin, Dennis Gaffney, Debby and David Flesher, Jude Rapheal, Mabel Maney, Polly Thistlethwaite, Burma Anderson, Jake Levich, and Victor and Lois Porlier. The enthusiasm, feedback, and literary camaraderie of each and every one of these kind and generous folks has had not only a welcomed ameliorating impact on the book, but on my life as well.

With these same warm sentiments, I'd also like to thank Barbara Kelly for her usual fastidious work in proofreading; Anne Dubuisson for her insightful editorial suggestions; Nancy Bereano of Firebrand Books for discussing the ins and outs of publishing; Susan Matthews of Stillwater Studio for production suggestions; and Paul Rapp, Esq. for his eagle eyes (and entertaining emails) during the legal review. The many participants on the PUBLISHERS-L listserve have also provided immense help to my thoughts about books and making books. Thanks also to Lissa D'Aquanni for marketing advice and gourmet chocolate; to Tina at the Karner Road Post Office for being the first non-family member to call me an "author," and to the folks at Upstates Independents for all their help and support; especially fellow writer Barbara Chepaitis for her enthusiasm and agent sharing, and Mike Camoin for his support.

I'd also like to thank everyone who ventured to the Bob Bridges Web site at www.bobbridges.com, and provided their discerning design comments on various incarnations of the book cover. Your help is much appreciated and remembered.

Although they may not have had so much to do directly with this particular book, I'd also like to thank various teachers I've had over the years for instilling in me a love of language and learning and for encouraging me along the way: Nita Groothuis, Ruth Geisking, Helen and Berel Lang, Howard DeLong, Helen Elam, Don Byrd, Jerome Rothenberg, Janet and Bill Grimes, and Jorge Klor de Alva, among many, many others.

Finally, no one can become a working artist without the support and encouragement of family and friends, and I would especially like to thank Chuck and Jon and everyone at Education 21 (Peter, Alannah, Georgia, Gerry, Kathy, and Cindy), Mom and Debby and David (and Lauren!), Grandpa Strawberry, Paula and Katie, Jill, Dennis and Kathy, Polly, Mabel, and most especially of all, that bewitching Irish she-devil, Debra.

About the Author

Penny Perkins was born in Vandalia, Illinois in 1962. She attended Trinity College in Hartford, CT, receiving an honors degree in philosophy. She also holds a Masters in English from the State University of New York at Albany. She has been a professional writer from more than 15 years, working in a variety of nonprofit agencies and holding several freelance positions. She is also the resident expert on Alternative Media for The Mining Co., posting weekly comentaries on the media at <http://altmedia.miningco.com>.

Bob Bridges is her first novel. She is currently working on a second novel and a screenplay.